D0207066

Drama Queen

candy apple books...
just for you.
sweet. fresh. fun.
take a bite!

Drama Queen

by LARA BERGEN

candy
Apple

SCHOLASTIC INC.

New York Toronto London Auckland Sydney
Mexico City New Delhi Hong Kong Buenos Aires

To the stars of my show:
Parker, Sydney & Stu

No part of this publication may be reproduced, stored in a retrieval system, or transmitted in any form or by any means, electronic, mechanical, photocopying, recording, or otherwise, without written permission of the publisher. For information regarding permission, write to Scholastic, Inc. Attention: Permissions Department, 557 Broadway, New York, NY 10012.

ISBN-13: 978-0-545-03751-8
ISBN-10: 0-545-03751-4

12 11 10 9 8 7 6 5 4 3 2 1   7 8 9 10 11 12/0
Printed in the U.S.A.   40
First printing, September 2007

Contents

Scene 1

Bigger School, Bigger Problems

"Don't look now!" the breathless voice behind Charlie warned. "And whatever you do, *don't* open that squeaky locker."

The voice belonged to Charlie's best friend since first grade, Nicole Bauer. The locker, unfortunately, belonged to Charlie.

"He's coming!" Nicole whispered.

As if on cue, Charlie and Nicole turned around as one and leaned against the cool metal doors behind them. "Hi, Kyle's" squeaked out of their throats a good three octaves higher than normal as the cutest boy in school — make that the whole *world* — walked toward them.

Charlie's eyes drank in every perfect strand of dark, wavy hair — the way it hung down perfectly over Kyle's perfect forehead, drawing her to his perfect blue eyes like a . . . like a . . . well, like a little sixth grade moth drawn to a perfectly perfect eighth grade flame. Charlie tried her best to block out the image of the scowling string bean beside him, otherwise known as her older brother, Sean.

As the girls held their breath, Kyle turned to acknowledge their squeaky greeting, then casually flipped his hair out of his eyes and flashed them a perfectly dimpled grin.

"Hey," he said.

Instantly, Charlie's stomach flip-flopped. As for the silly grin on her face, she was incapable of controlling it and didn't even bother to try.

Out of habit more than anything, a "hi" tumbled out of her lips in the direction of her brother. But the last thing he wanted was to be caught chatting with his little sister. And that was fine. Sean kept Kyle moving — which meant Charlie and Nicole could turn back around and breathe.

"I swear, you are the luckiest girl in school!" Nicole told Charlie as soon as Kyle was out of earshot. "I mean, not only do you live on Kyle's street, but your brother is his best friend." She sighed a deep, dreamy, oh-if-only-I-were-you sigh. "So, how's their band doing?"

"You mean the Hot Pockets?"

Nicole frowned. "I thought it was the Pop-Tarts."

Charlie shook her head. "It was, but Sean changed it *again*."

Nicole giggled.

"Don't laugh. They were almost called the Pizza Egg Rolls. It was Sean's favorite food for an hour, I think. Not that he actually tells me anything. And not that he ever lets me anywhere near him and Kyle." Charlie turned back to her locker and groaned. "He's probably told him all kinds of horrible things about me. It's the curse of being his sister, I guess."

"It's still better than nothing," said Nicole, who included "no older brothers with cute friends" on her Top Ten List of Reasons Why It Stinks to Be an Only Child. Charlie was constantly amazed that after all these years around Charlie's crazy family, Nicole still couldn't see how lucky she was. She had a huge house and her mom and dad all to herself. *Plus* she was tall and had naturally curly hair. All the things Charlie dreamed of!

"Well, is the band practicing today?" Nicole went on. "I mean, maybe I could come over later."

"Don't bother," said Charlie. "My mom is teaching Tuesday and Thursday afternoons this semester, so I promised I'd babysit Olivia those days. I think Sean has some guitar lesson or something, and Jen and Gwen have cheerleading. I get paid . . . but it's still a pain. Plus I've got to memorize that poem for English, *if* Olivia will let me. Maybe you could come over on Friday . . ."

Or maybe, if she was lucky, sometime after college graduation.

It was funny. All her life Charlie had wanted to grow up. To go to the bigger schools her big brother and sisters went to. To babysit and make real money. To wear makeup.

What had she been thinking?

One month into junior high and it was all becoming clear. A bigger school just meant bigger problems! Like bigger homework assignments — huge, enormous, mind-draining, afternoon-eating homework assignments. Not to mention about a thousand more kids to worry about fitting in with!

And what had ever made her think that *babysitting* would be fun? Especially when it involved her own six-year-old sister, Olivia, who was utterly incapable of leaving Charlie alone for a second. If you asked Charlie, no amount of money was worth it. Particularly when she had no time left to spend it.

As for makeup — that was still a *long* way off, or so her mother said.

Charlie slowly turned her combination lock to the third and final number. Then she yanked hard on the locker door. Yep, growing up was definitely overrat —

"What is that noise?"

Charlie winced as the piercing squeak of her locker hinges ricocheted through the hall, along the speckled floor, and off the glossy heads of a pack of perfectly *awful* eighth grade girls.

"Oh, no," groaned Nicole, shutting her own locker door and dropping her head. "How many times do I have to tell you to bring in some WD-40 for that thing?"

"I know," muttered Charlie, sticking her beet-red face into her open locker. Really, she'd bring it the next day. But that wasn't going to help her live through this one. . . .

"Seriously!" said the red-haired girl leading the group of eighth graders. She covered her ears with her hands. "It sounds like someone's being *tortured!*"

"Yeah, *us!*" said another.

"Totally!" The first girl laughed almost hard enough to make her pre-ripped jeans split more, which prompted the others to dissolve into a chorus of nasty laughter. Then, as if she had sixth-grader-seeking radar, the redhead zeroed in on Charlie, who had made the fatal error of meekly turning around.

"Maybe you don't know any better, but you need to get that thing fixed. If not for you, then for the sake of others." The girl smiled down at Charlie with the warmth of a vulture all too happy to eat her guts out. Then she glanced back at her friends and basked in their approving giggles.

"Come on," she said, tossing her head and turning away. "Let's go before she closes her locker."

The girls bounced off, snickering, and disappeared around a corner. Charlie quickly turned around and buried her head back in her locker. Fortunately, the rest of the kids in the hall seemed to be going about their business. Still, Charlie had already decided she wasn't moving until the bell rang.

Nicole, however, was seething.

"Just *who* does she think she is?" she snarled through her new braces, glaring at the space where the red-haired girl had been.

"I think," said Charlie, "she thinks she's Amber Wiley."

"You know her?" Nicole asked.

"I know who she *is*," Charlie said. "Sean talks about her. He thinks she's cute. She wanted to sing in his band, but he said, 'No girls,' so she doesn't talk to him anymore. I don't know who's better off."

"*He* is," growled Nicole. "She can't treat people the way she just treated you!"

"Oh, forget about it," said Charlie. "I promise, I'll fix my locker tomorrow, and we'll never have to deal with Amber Wiley again."

Just then, the bell rang and the hall began to clear.

"Charlie!" said Nicole, tugging hard on Charlie's hunched shoulder. "C'mon, we've gotta go!"

Quickly, Charlie grabbed every book she'd need for the rest of the day, gave her squeaky locker a good, stiff kick, and hurried off to chorus.

Scene 2

The Announcement

Chorus was definitely the high point of Charlie's day. She liked a lot of her classes, sure. They were interesting and usually painless. But chorus was actually *fun*. There were no tricky questions or ten-page papers to write, no competition for the highest score on some quiz, nobody swearing they *never* studied when they always got straight A's. Just a roomful of voices. It was the one period where Charlie could relax and feel like she belonged.

Plus, there was never any homework!

Charlie gave a "later" wave to Nicole, who was an alto, and slipped into her seat at the back of the soprano section. Mr. Matthews, the chorus teacher, had just finished taking roll.

"Glad you could make it, Miss Bauer and Miss Moore," he said, pulling down his glasses to shoot each of them his Look — which, despite his bushy, bunched-up brow, always came across as more amused than stern. Charlie, in fact, had never seen Mr. Matthews look anything other than terribly pleased to be there. She grinned apologetically at him.

"Now," Mr. Matthews went on, closing his roll book and stepping around to the front of the podium. "I'm eager to begin this new piece we've been working on, but before we warm up and start singing, I want to talk to you all about the fall musical. A sign-up sheet went up outside the drama room yesterday, and there's not a single sixth grade name on it yet."

He held up his hands in a *what gives?* gesture, as half-curious murmurs wafted about the room.

"Come on, guys. Auditions are Friday. There's no reason that every single one of you shouldn't be there."

Charlie caught Nicole's eye from across the room. She could tell Nicole was interested. Charlie wasn't so sure about the whole thing, however. She loved singing in a group . . . and in church . . . and in the shower. But in a costume in front of the whole school?

"Why bother?" one boy in the tenors called out. "Sixth graders never get good parts."

"Well, first of all," replied Mr. Matthews, "'good part' is a relative term. What would a musical be without a chorus to support it? I always thought it was the most fun part of a show. But secondly, I happen to think this is one of the most talented sixth grade classes we've had in years. I wouldn't be surprised if one or more of you got a lead."

As he spoke, his eyes traveled in Charlie's direction. She glanced over her shoulder to see who was behind her, but there was just the wall. She turned back around. Was Mr. Matthews — *gulp* — looking at *her*?

A really nice girl named Megan, who sat next to Charlie, raised her hand. "What's the show going to be?" she asked.

Mr. Matthews rubbed his hands together. "*Robin Hood*! Sounds like fun, doesn't it?"

Charlie had to smile. Yeah, it kind of did.

Naturally, there were groans from the usual groaners in the class, along with a fair amount of excited chatter.

Mr. Matthews grinned. "Now let me just see a show of hands. Who's on board for these auditions?"

Here and there around the room, a dozen hands drifted up to form a meager crop of volunteers.

Charlie's hand hovered hesitantly under her chin, despite Nicole's enthusiastic arm pumps and insistent stares.

It was just that Charlie had so much else to *do*. She wondered how much work a junior high musical involved. Where would she ever find the time? Between her endless list of chores (which her mom seemed all too eager to add to daily) and the general constant chaos of a house full of five kids (four of whom were completely annoying), she barely had time to do her homework.

The Look made its way back to Mr. Matthews' face. "By the way," he said dryly, "did I mention that everyone who tries out for the show will get extra credit?"

Like rockets, all arms — including Charlie's — shot into the air.

"Wonderful!" said Mr. Matthews. "Now, open your songbooks and let's begin."

Well into the second song of the day, a piece of tightly folded notebook paper made its way (with the help of many willing and dutiful shoes) across the dusty linoleum tiles of the back row to Charlie's Vans.

Glancing down, she could see her name spelled out in Nicole's big loopy writing. And so, as soon as she was *pretty* sure Mr. Matthews wasn't looking, she cautiously reached down, grabbed the note, and opened it up.

Dear C,

I have to leave after 5th period to go to the orthodontist (aka House of Pain) — but promise you'll meet me by the drama sign-up sheet before homeroom tomorrow morning. First thing! We are sooooo doing that audition! Together!

Do not wimp out! I know where you live!

I mean it,

N.

P.S. Guess what! Emily went to the musical last year with her sister and says it was really good. But guess who the star was? Amber Wiley! Emily says she can really sing. (And she knows it!) Think she'll do it again?

P.P.S. Very important! Don't forget to find out when the Hot Tarts (cute, right?) are practicing. Please! Please! Please!!!!!

Still mouthing the words of the song the group was singing (or something close to them), Charlie carefully folded the note back up.

Okay. So that was that. They were auditioning.

Really, Charlie knew, there was no other choice when Nicole's mind was made up. Charlie would go along with it — and that was fine. Maybe it would even be fun.

But not if *Amber Wiley* was going to be in the show, too!

Charlie's lips froze midsyllable. Her eyes widened and shot across the room toward Nicole. They were quickly intercepted, however, by Mr. Matthews' Look.

"Miss Moore," he said. "You look distracted. Is something wrong?"

"Uh . . ." Charlie mumbled something indecipherable and weakly shook her head.

"Did you hit a bad *note,* perhaps?"

As he spoke the words, the corners of Mr. Matthews' mouth twitched playfully, and Charlie was pretty sure that he'd been watching her all along.

Charlie groaned quietly. She'd been caught with a note in her English class already, the week before, and had to read it out loud. Luckily, it had only been about a homework assignment. Honestly, if she had to read a note out loud again in chorus, there was an *extremely* good chance that would be the last day she ever showed her face in Roosevelt Junior High.

She held her breath. . . .

"Not to worry, Miss Moore," he went on. "I heard it, too. But I think we can work through it." The Look flashed across his face again — but only for a moment. "We've got so much going for us. I don't think we'll be hearing it anymore after this class, do you?"

Charlie relaxed as a cool wave of relief washed over her.

"No, Mr. Matthews," she replied.

"Fantastic. So, class, let's see if we can run through this last part one more time before —"

BRRRINNNNGGGG!

"— the bell rings. Ah, well."

The shuffling of feet and excited chatter rose in a chorus, quickly taking over the room.

Like everyone else, Charlie scooped up her books and made for the door, but not before offering Mr. Matthews a grateful smile.

He smiled back. "Thank you, sixth grade, for another inspiring hour. And remember," he hollered over the noise, "get those names down on the audition sheet! I want to see each and every one of your shining faces there on Friday. Have a great afternoon!"

Scene 3
Home Sweet Home?

The rest of the day went about as expected: Leo Watson, Charlie's lab partner, made her do all the work in science; Ms. Pappas, her math teacher, gave out *way* too much homework; and not one single person thought to tell Charlie that there was a big smear of blue ink across her nose through most of English. (If only Nicole hadn't had to leave early! She would have had Charlie's back.)

Charlie was more than glad when the final bell rang and it was time, at last, to go home.

It was a short walk home, past the elementary school and around another corner. If she was really running late in the morning, Charlie could leave the house when the first bell rang and be through her homeroom door *just* before the late bell. But going home, she liked to take her time.

When she reached her front door, Charlie fished for her key in her backpack and slipped it into the lock.

Click.

CRRREEEEAK.

What was it with her and squeaky doors?

She pushed open the door and listened for a moment. *Ah.* The sweet sound of silence. It was not a sound heard in Charlie's house very often, and she paused to let it sink in.

She glanced at the clock above the hall table. 2:45. She had twenty minutes — maybe twenty-five — to revel in life as an only child, and she wasn't going to waste it.

Slipping off her shoes, Charlie dashed into the kitchen and poked her head into the pantry. Yes! The box of Oreos was still there! She pulled the box out and hungrily reached in. It was empty. Typical!

She surveyed her options again. Chocolate chip cookies? Empty. Her favorite cereal? Empty. Graham crackers? *Please?* Empty.

With a huff, she left the boxes where they were (whoever finished them could throw them out!) and moved on to the fridge, where she settled for the last fat-free raspberry yogurt. She grabbed the carton and a (hopefully) clean spoon from the dish rack and headed for the living room.

Of course, Charlie knew there was no time to really *watch* anything. Honestly, all she cared about was the sheer pleasure of holding the remote in her hand and flipping through channels of her own choosing.

She clicked on the TV and started channel-surfing.

Look! A cheerleading competition on the sports channel . . .

Bor-*ing! Click.*

Well, what do you know? A music video by her brother's favorite band . . .

Who cares? Click.

How cute! That show her sister loved that wasn't *Barney* but might as well be . . .

P-*lease! Click.*

Hmm . . . , thought Charlie as she clicked through a few more no-gos. *Maybe I should see what's on the classic movie channel. What's that? Nobody else likes old movies? It's not my turn to pick a show? Oh, really?* Too bad!

She punched in channel 54 and watched as a cast of characters appeared in Technicolor on the screen. *Hey!* The Adventures of Robin Hood. *Cool!*

Charlie remembered this part; it was probably halfway through the movie. Maid Marian was in her tower room, wearing a dreamy silver gown, as Robin Hood was leaping through the window, sweeping her off her dainty feet. Could there be, in the whole world, anything more romantic than that?

Maybe, thought Charlie, *this is a sign.* She hadn't been so sure about trying out for the school show. But perhaps she was meant to!

She lay back on the sofa, turned up the volume, and tried to imagine herself in lamé and ropes of pearls, just like Maid Marian. . . .

CRRREEEEAK!

SLAM!

"Hey! I hear the TV! Mom said no TV! I'm telling Mom the TV was on! I'm hungry! And so is Nelson!"

Charlie sighed and punched the Off button. Her sister Olivia was home.

Olivia was six — going on *three*. Oh, she could talk just fine. She could even read. And she was taller than most kids in her class. The problem, in fact, wasn't even with Olivia. It was with her best friend, a fine fellow named Nelson. An utterly fine, utterly *invisible* fellow named Nelson.

"We want cookies," Olivia declared, rifling

through the pantry as Charlie walked into the kitchen.

"There aren't any," said Charlie.

"I see boxes."

"They're empty."

Olivia went to the fridge. "What about yogurt?"

"No yogurt, either."

Olivia turned around. "Did you eat it all?" she demanded.

Charlie put her hands on her hips. "Maybe," she said.

"That's not fair! I'm telling Mom!"

"Olivia," Charlie huffed, "I have a lot of homework to do. Tell me what you want to eat — that we actually have — right now, or you'll have to get it yourself."

Olivia held her hand up to her mouth and conferred with Nelson (otherwise known as the air).

"We'd like some ants on a log." She jerked to the left as if someone incredibly strong had nudged her. *"Please."*

"Okay," Charlie said. At least Nelson had some manners. She got out the peanut butter and the bag of raisins. "Want to grab the celery?"

Happily, Olivia reached back into the fridge, pulled out a big bunch of celery (which she proudly showed to Nelson), and handed it to Charlie.

"Don't forget to make two," she reminded Charlie. "One for Nelson, and one for me."

Charlie rolled her eyes and broke off four long stalks. While she was at it, she might as well make extras. Ants on a log was actually one of her favorites, and she was secretly glad that Olivia (and Nelson) liked it, too.

Charlie glanced over at her sister. "I thought Mom said Nelson wasn't supposed to go to school with you anymore."

Olivia twirled her blond hair around her finger. "He doesn't," she mumbled, casting downward glances. "He waits for me up at the top of the flagpole." She winked and giggled. "Don'tcha, Nelson? Between the state flag and the American one. I can see him from my classroom."

Man, thought Charlie. *No wonder my sister doesn't have many friends. She's certifiably wacko! Or is she just trying to drive me crazy?*

She dropped the raisin ants, one by one, in neat rows along the peanut butter–covered logs. She debated whether to make up one plate or two for her sister, but decided to give her two, to avoid any further discussion. She set them down on the counter by Olivia's stool.

"Not there, silly!" Olivia scolded. "Nelson's over there." She pointed to the kitchen table.

Charlie glared at her sister. "*You* move it," she told her. Then she chomped down on her own celery stick and headed out of the room. "Make sure you and *Nelson* put the plates in the sink when you're done!" she called over her shoulder. "I have homework to do."

"But, Charlie!" she heard Olivia call back. "Nelson wants you to play a game. Remember? Mom said you would!"

There were hours, Charlie thought, and then there were *hours* . . . long, excruciating units of three thousand six hundred mind-numbing seconds, with no end. These were the hours she spent babysitting Olivia.

You'd think with a 24/7 built-in friend, Olivia would be able to entertain herself. But no. Having Nelson around just meant more work for Charlie. More snacks to make, of course. More pages to help color. (Being invisible, Nelson preferred invisible crayons, as well — but Olivia insisted that Charlie help him as best she could.) And more stories to read. ("It's not fair," said Olivia, "to let one of us pick a story and not the other!")

And then there were board games, which

Charlie avoided like the plague. Waiting for Nelson to take his turn was *torture*!

Really, Charlie told herself, her mom should pay her double. Maybe she'd ask her about it when she got home from work.

Yeah, right!

"Okay," Charlie told Olivia when they'd finally finished playing Sorry!, "I have to memorize this poem for school tonight. If you want, you can sit here *silently* while I do. Otherwise, you're on your own until Mom gets home."

"Hmm . . ." Olivia thought for a moment. "What's the poem about?"

Before Charlie could answer, however, the front door flew open and a whirl of arms and legs and bouncy hair blew into the room.

"H-E-double-L-O! We're home! We're home! *We're home!*"

"Hi, Gwen," said Charlie. "Hi, Jen."

Gwen and Jen were Charlie's older sisters: identical twins, juniors in high school — and, yes, cheerleaders.

From the curly ribbons in their perky blond ponytails to the laces in their blinding white shoes, they looked and dressed exactly alike. Most people couldn't tell them apart. But Charlie could, no problem. Gwen's teeth were bigger, and Jen's pierced ears were totally uneven.

"Was there a game today?" asked Charlie, eyeing their blue-and-gold pleated skirts.

"Nah," the twins said. "We just wanted to show some spirit!"

"Let's hear it for spirit!"

They laughed and pumped their arms and bobbed around in place.

"So," Jen turned to Charlie and Olivia. "We're here! We're near! And we're ready to cheer!"

"Yeah, sorry guys," said Gwen. "We're totally going to need this room to practice."

Charlie couldn't believe it. "I thought you were just *at* practice?"

"Hell-*o*," said Jen, rolling her eyes. "It's football season!"

"Seriously," said Gwen. "Like three hours of practice is enough. For the football players, maybe." She turned to Jen and laughed. "But we have, like, twenty different routines to do *per game*!"

"Well, can't you practice somewhere else, like in your room?" said Charlie, who didn't want to give up her prime seat on the couch.

"Uh, no," said Gwen and Jen together. They bent their knees, then sprang up in a series of pikes and tucks and various other unnatural positions. "We need room to do our jumps."

"Well, how 'bout outside?" Charlie said. "I mean, we were here first." She held her hand out toward Olivia (and Nelson). "And you know, technically, that's three against two."

Jen pulled a DVD out of her bag and smiled. "We have to watch *this*."

Charlie reached into her own bag and pulled out the poem she had to memorize. "We're not leaving."

"Suit yourself," said Jen, popping the disc into the DVD player.

Charlie looked over at Olivia, who was slipping out of the room. "Where are you going?" she asked.

"Nelson wants to go up to our room," Olivia said. She put a hand up to her mouth and pointed with her other finger at Gwen and Jen. "He's scared of them," she whispered. Then she turned and hurried up the stairs.

"Ready? Begin!"

One, two, three, four, who's the team that's gonna score?
Five, six, seven, eight, Titans! Titans! We're great, great, GREAT!
Goooooo, Titans!

Charlie buried her face in her poem. *Great,* she thought. *This is just GREAT.* She could sit here, without the slightest hope of memorizing one lousy word. Or she could go up to the room she shared with Olivia — and commiserate with Nelson!

What was the point of a person with four siblings even *trying* to do homework?

Finally, after enduring the dozenth cheer, Charlie stalked out of the living room toward the kitchen. It wasn't the most comfortable place to work, but it was the best chance she had of concentra —

That's when Charlie ran into someone.

Someone named — *gulp!* — Kyle.

Scene 4
Huge News

It wasn't every day that the cutest boy in school walked through your front door, but thanks to Charlie's brother, Sean, it did happen at least once or twice a week.

"What's up, dork?" said Sean as he followed Kyle through the front door. "Out of our way, already."

"Sean!" said their mother, who was bringing up the rear. "You absolutely may not speak to your sister that way! Hi, sweetie. How was your day? How was Olivia?"

Charlie shrugged. "Well, ac —"

"Sean! Pick up your coat, please. Don't just leave it there! Were you raised in a barn?"

It was a known fact in the Moore house that, no matter how sincere the question, by the time their mom asked one thing, she'd be on to something else. Under no circumstances was an answer ever required.

"Excuse me, guys," Charlie's mom went on, heading toward the kitchen with two bulging shopping bags. "I need to get this food in the fridge. Anyone want to help me? Sean, put that guitar away, also. Kyle, are you staying for dinner?"

Kyle, who knew the drill, saved his answer and gave it to Charlie with a dimpled half grin and a shake of his head. He casually flipped his hair toward his house down the street. "Gotta get home soon," he said. Or at least that's what Charlie thought he said. It was kind of hard to tell when her ears kept ringing, just from being in the same room with him.

Sean picked up his jacket and his guitar and rolled his eyes. The eye roll, of course, was for Kyle's benefit. But Kyle's eyes had kept moving, past Charlie, toward the living room, from which cheers were still erupting.

Hey, hey, Titan fans,
Yell it out and rock the stands!

"Er . . . um . . . so . . ." Charlie swallowed in an effort to get some moisture back in her mouth. "Are you guys gonna practice right now?" she finally mumbled.

"None of your business," Sean snapped back. Charlie couldn't help noticing his particularly sour tone. "But if you have to know, no!" he went on. "Right, Kyle?"

"What? Huh?" Reluctantly, Kyle freed himself momentarily from the spell of the Moore twins' cheers. "Oh, right. Gotta take a break, man. No band practice for a while."

No doubt about it!
Stand up and shout it!

Charlie could see that her brother was seething. And even though she was troubled by the news, she couldn't help enjoying the sight.

"What happened?" she asked. Had Kyle finally figured out what a pain in the neck her brother was? Had he decided he didn't want to sing in a band called the Hot Pockets or the Tuna Melts or the PBJs?

"Get this," Sean said, shaking his head in utter disgust. "He wants to do that lame school musical. Can you believe it?"

Charlie's eyes grew wide. She wasn't sure what surprised her more — the fact that her brother had just willingly given her information or that Kyle was going to try out for the show, too. Now *that* was big news!

"The school musical is not lame," Kyle said. "No lamer than you, anyway. You should do it, man. Then you'd know."

"Are you kidding?" said Sean, as if he'd been asked to dance around the kitchen in a tutu. "I don't act, and I sure don't sing."

Kyle rolled his eyes jokingly. "You got that right. But you don't have to act or sing. You could play your guitar in the orchestra."

"Whatever," Sean said, shrugging the absurd idea away. (In her own mind, Charlie wiped her brow with relief.)

"Yeah, whatever," said Kyle. Then he grinned and somehow his eyes found their way back to Charlie. "You're at Roosevelt now," he said with a nod that made Charlie swoon. "You should try out, too."

Charlie's face got so red so fast it actually hurt. Or maybe it was the smile stretched too tightly across her cheeks.

She opened her mouth. "Do you . . . do you really think I should?"

"Okay, enough of this drama talk," Sean said

quickly, steering Kyle away. "Let's play 'Guitar Hero II.' You want to?"

"Sweet," said Kyle. He turned to wink at Charlie as if to say, "Sean has no idea what he's talking about," then fell in step with Sean. "Sure your sisters won't mind?" he asked.

"Who cares?" said Sean.

Charlie stood there for a moment, half reliving her conversation with Kyle (she could call it that, couldn't she?) and half listening to Jen and Gwen shower him with attention.

Give me a K!
Give me a Y!
Give me an L!
Give me an E!
That's the way we spell it.
Here's the way we yell it!

Give me a B-R-E-A-K, thought Charlie. She wished her too-cute sisters would flirt with someone their own age. Really!

But there was no time to waste. What had just happened wasn't something you kept to yourself. These were events to be shared! She hurried to the kitchen and grabbed the phone.

"Did you finish your homework?" Mom asked,

glancing up from something leafy and green in the sink.

"Uh —"

"Hungry?" Mom asked, looking down once again. "I hope so; I've got a lot of this stuff."

Phone in hand, Charlie ducked out of the kitchen, then paused to consider the best place for a private call. . . . Kitchen? No. Living room? No. Bedroom? No. Basement? Damp, dark, cold. Yes. Thank goodness for the quiet basement.

Charlie opened the door and flicked the switch, and the one bare bulb came on. Then she pulled the door shut behind her and took a cold, hard seat on the dusty bottom stair. She punched Nicole's number into the phone.

"— so we totally think a Herkie works best for the 'Hello' cheer. It's so, like, perfect. You'll love it. Hey? Is someone on the other line? Hello? Hello?"

Charlie frowned and quickly punched End.

No way, she thought. Somehow Jen had beaten her to the phone. Well, one thing was for sure. That call would last forever! Maybe Nicole was online.

Charlie ran up out of the basement and across the hall to her mom's office. There were computers in each of their rooms, but only their mom's had Internet access.

Anyway, this would just be one quick e-mail —

maybe an IM, if Charlie was lucky. Charlie opened the door, already composing the message in her mind. Nicole was going to go crazy!

"Hell-o! Haven't you ever heard of knocking?"

"What? Gwen? What are you —"

"Cheer chat," said Gwen, quickly typing something, then uttering a short, high laugh. Then she looked up at Charlie. "I totally meant to ask you — isn't it time to go out for cheerleading at Roosevelt? You know, Coach Farrell loves us. With just a little training, we could totally get you on the team."

Charlie shook her head. Was Gwen kidding?

"Thanks, Gwen," she said. "But I totally don't think so." Then she stepped back out of the room and closed the door.

Running low on options, Charlie headed for the kitchen. "Mom," she called, "can I use your cell phone?"

Her mom was flipping back and forth through the pages of a cookbook: *The Working Mother's Guide to Delicious Meals in Minutes*. (Minutes that, unfortunately, usually ran into the triple digits.)

"I forgot to buy shallots!" her mother groaned. Her cell phone sat on the counter by the stove.

"Mom?" said Charlie. "Just for a minute?"

Her mom looked up and waved her wooden

spoon. "Haven't I told you that my phone is not a toy?" she asked.

"I don't want to play with it," Charlie said flatly. "Jen's on the house phone and Gwen's on the computer, and I have something really, *really* important to tell Nicole."

Her mom almost looked sorry. "Actually, honey, I'm waiting for a call from school. I might have to sub for a class in the morning if they can't find anyone else. You understand, don't you?"

Yeah, thought Charlie. She understood. She understood that when it came to her place in this family, she was about as close to the bottom as she could possibly be. Even Olivia got to tell her what to do now that she was babysitting her.

What she wouldn't give to be an only child and have her *own* phone, like Nicole! It just wasn't fair.

"Hey, Charlie," her mom called to her. "Why don't you go tell Jen and Gwen they have to come and set the table?" She smiled. "Then you can use the phone, or the Internet, or whatever you like. Okay?"

Charlie smiled back. "Okay."

Scene 5

Signing Up

By the next day, it was settled. No doubt about it. Charlie was signing up for musical auditions with Nicole. They met, as planned, outside the drama room before homeroom and stared at the sign-up sheet — all eleven by fourteen inches of it — just waiting for their names.

"Hey!" Nicole said. "I don't see Kyle's name on here yet."

"Are you sure?" Charlie said.

"Yeah. Take a look."

Charlie's eyes scanned the list of a dozen or so names, most of which she'd never heard before, and she frowned.

"I hope your brother didn't talk him out of it," Nicole said.

"Me too," Charlie said as doubt tiptoed through her brain. "I mean, he seemed really serious about it yesterday. . . ."

"Well," said Nicole, trying to stay optimistic, "maybe he just hasn't had a chance yet. It's only the middle of the week."

"Hi, guys!" said a voice behind them.

Charlie turned and saw Megan and a few more kids from chorus approaching.

"Did you sign up? We're going to, too!"

"Oh, good," said Charlie. "I was getting a little worried that we wouldn't know anyone."

Megan walked up to the list and signed her name. "Well, now you do!" she said. She handed the pen to her friend Claire. "I'm so glad Mr. Matthews told us about the musical. I had no idea."

"*I'm* glad we get extra credit!" said Claire. Then her hand suddenly froze. "You do think he was serious about that, don't you?"

"He'd better be!" said another girl, Lily. "Now, hurry up and write your name down."

Soon there were seven more sixth graders on the list, and a bunch more kids waiting to add their names. Arden, an alto, like Nicole, handed her the pen. "Your turn," she said. "What role do you want?"

Nicole signed her name. "Well, Maid Marian, of

course," she said. "But I'll play anything. Even a boy!" She passed the pen to Charlie. "What about you?"

Charlie laughed and shrugged. "Who knows if I'll get a part at all?"

"Oh, you definitely will," said Megan. "You are *such* a good singer."

"Ycah, you really are," said Claire.

Charlie grinned as she dotted her *i.* "Thanks," she mumbled, suddenly self-conscious but flattered. *You know,* she thought, *even if Kyle doesn't try out, this could really be fun. . . .*

"Well, well, well. If it isn't Squeaky Locker Girl! Going to try out for the musical? I hope you sound better than that locker of yours. Or do you plan on torturing us that way, too?"

The dot on Charlie's *i* turned into a long, tortured slash as her hand slipped halfway down the page. She didn't turn around to see who belonged to the haughty voice behind her — or the laughs that followed. She didn't have to.

"Let's see," said Amber Wiley, walking up to the list and elbowing Charlie out of the way. She studied the sign-up sheet closely. " 'Charlie Moore.' Oh, sure! You're one of Sean's sisters." She turned and looked at her friends like she'd just smelled something awful. "I think *all* these little sixth graders signed up, guys. Can you believe it? What songs do you think they'll audition with? The Wiggles?"

She gave her friends a second to appreciate her wit, then turned back to Charlie. "*You'll* probably sing one of your brother's lame songs, though, won't you?"

Charlie looked back at Amber without the slightest idea of what to say. The thing was, she agreed with her. Her brother's songs *were* lame. Except maybe for the one about peace and love. She didn't know where that one had come from. But it was pretty good.

"Oh, whatever," said Amber, finally seeming to tire of making fun of Charlie for the moment. "Do you mind?" She held out her hand and tapped her foot impatiently.

Charlie stared back at her blankly.

"The *pen!*" Amber said as if Charlie were two years old. "I know, you probably don't think I *need* to audition, having starred in the last two shows. But it's a formality. So hand it over. Eighth graders can't be late, you know. Our classes are very important."

More than happy to hand over the pen (and get as far from Amber as possible), Charlie offered it up willingly and slunk back into the crowd.

"*Thank* you," said Amber, flipping her red hair

as she turned to face the sign-up sheet. She added her name to the very top of the growing list.

But Nicole wasn't about to stand back and watch. "You know," she said, stepping up and planting her feet on the floor behind Amber. "There's no need to talk to people that way."

Amber spun around. "Excuse me?" she said, chuckling.

"You heard me," said Nicole.

"No, I didn't," said Amber. Her eyes narrowed. "Say it again. I *dare* you."

Charlie had to grin. *She dares her?* she thought. This was going to be good. Nicole hadn't passed up a dare since second grade.

Nicole put her hands on her hips and made the most of the six inches she had on the older girl. "You," Nicole declared, "are just plain —"

Suddenly, Nicole's jaw went slack — but it wasn't because of Amber.

Like the Red Sea parting, the whole cluster of girls stepped back to allow His Royal Cuteness, Kyle, to drift through. Their eyes trailed him as he made his way to the list. Even Amber was dumbstruck — for a split second.

"Kyle!" she said, quickly regaining her composure. "Oh, good! Are you signing up, too?"

Kyle shrugged and coolly nodded, taking time to flash a friendly grin at each and every girl around him. "Yeah."

For the first time in her life, Charlie saw real live human eyelashes actually flutter. "We should rehearse together for the audition!" cooed Amber.

Kyle shrugged again. "Yeah, maybe." He looked at the sign-up sheet, then glanced around for a second, saw the pen in Amber's hand, and reached into his pocket. He pulled out a nubby pencil and loosely wrote his name down on the sheet.

"I'll call you!" said Amber as Kyle began to walk away.

"Yeah," he said. Then, without so much as a warning — without the slightest indication at all — Kyle did something amazing. He stopped in front of Charlie.

"Hey." He smiled and nodded toward the sign-up sheet. "Cool. You signed up."

Through sheer determination, Charlie willed herself not to faint as her stomach, lungs, and liver — and maybe her spleen, too — wedged themselves in her throat.

A horrible thought flashed suddenly through her brain: could people explode?

Fortunately, Kyle's eyes lifted off her as quickly

as they'd landed, pausing for another moment on an unsuspecting Nicole.

"And your friend, too. See you guys at the auditions."

He displayed a set of perfectly perfect teeth and drifted down the hall.

Charlie and Nicole turned to each other without even trying to contain their delight. Amber didn't try to contain her feelings, either. Her eyes widened. Her jaw dropped. She stared after Kyle, unmoving.

Life is just full of beautiful surprises, Charlie thought. *Eat your heart out, Amber!*

Scene 6

Home Sweet Home (for Real)

"Honestly," said Nicole. "I couldn't believe the look on Amber's face!"

"I know," said Charlie, grinning. "It was great!"

What was also great was an afternoon away from crazy Casa Moore. It was the twins' turn to watch Olivia, and Charlie was on her way to Nicole's house. It was the perfect end to a rather awesome day. She'd aced her poem recitation, watched a movie in social studies, and, of course, had her moment with Kyle!

Instead of walking, Nicole rode the bus — which *she* wasn't crazy about but Charlie loved. First of all, Noah and Eric, the funniest kids in their class, rode the bus, too. They were always good for a few laughs. Second, Nicole's bus driver, Mrs. Hill, was by far the nicest person Charlie had ever met. And finally, Nicole lived on the bumpiest, windiest, steepest road in the world, and riding down it on a school bus was about as close to riding a roller coaster as a person could get on a daily basis.

"Look out! I'm going to throw up! It's coming your way, Charlie!" Noah cried.

"Incoming!" Eric said, laughing and ducking.

Well, maybe they weren't *always* funny.

The bus zoomed down a hill and stopped halfway up the next one to drop off Nicole and Charlie.

"Have a good afternoon, girls," Mrs. Hill said as they stepped off. "It was so nice to see you, Charlie." She winked and waved, then pulled the lever to close the door. "Boys, sit down back there, please."

As the bus slowly pulled away, Charlie waved to Eric and Noah, who were now seated and making faces out the back window. Then Nicole led the way down the driveway to her house.

To Charlie, Nicole's house was truly perfect in every way. It was old and huge (verging on a mansion, if you asked Charlie), with all kinds of rooms, and rooms off rooms. It even had a few extra staircases, which Nicole said had been for servants years and years ago!

When they were little, Charlie would come over and make Nicole play hide-and-seek with her *all the time*. And to be honest, she *still* would have enjoyed a game. There was no end to the secret places you could find in Nicole's house. But there were other pleasures to be found, too: homemade cookies, brownies, and an endless selection of snacks, lined up in neat rows of unripped boxes that were never, *ever* empty when you reached in for a handful; an honest-to-goodness grand piano that Nicole's mom had inherited from her favorite aunt; a computer *with* e-mail right in Nicole's room; and a big-screen TV *with* TiVo all to themselves.

Charlie followed Nicole through the door and hung her jacket on the old wooden coatrack in the hall. A warm bundle of fur coiled itself around her ankles — Nicole's cat, Dr. Pepper. Charlie bent down and scooped him up while Nicole walked over to the wide, curving staircase.

"Hi, Mom!" she hollered. "We're home!"

"Hi, hon. Hi, Charlie," her mom called back. "I'll be down in a sec. Just finishing this article. There's a surprise in the kitchen for you two. Help yourselves!"

Nicole rubbed her hands together and led Charlie into the kitchen. On the counter was a plate piled high with chocolate chip Rice Krispies Treats.

"All *right*!" said Nicole.

Charlie nuzzled Dr. Pepper's head, then lowered him to the floor. She picked up a sticky Rice Krispies Treat and took a bite. "Good," she said. "But I think I like the ones she dipped in chocolate even better."

"Yeah," Nicole agreed, already reaching for a second. "Those are Dad's favorites, too."

"So, what's your mom working on?" Charlie asked, licking her fingers.

Nicole thought for a sec. "I think it's an article about parenting, or maybe one about midlife crises." She shrugged. "I'm not sure. Those are her usual topics, anyway. She'll probably read it to me tonight."

Nicole walked over to the fridge and got them each a drink. "Hey, I have an idea!" she said. "Let's go on the computer and look up some songs for our audition. The sign said we had to have a song prepared to sing, right?"

Charlie nodded. "Yeah. I was thinking we'd just sing something from chorus, though."

Nicole waved the ridiculous concept away. "No, no, *no*! Half the class will do that. We have to set ourselves apart!" She stopped and grinned. "Well, at least I do. You're so good, you could probably sing anything. I'll bet you get a lead." She closed her eyes and smiled dreamily. "Ah, yes. I can just see you now, singing and dancing your way through Sherwood Forest, arm in arm with Kyle. . . ."

"I *wish*!" Charlie said. Then she sighed. "Or maybe I don't. I mean, I have to say, this whole musical is a *lot* less appealing now that Amber Wiley's involved."

"I know!" Nicole moaned. "But really, Charlie. I hear she picks on everybody — and you're a way better singer than her."

"I don't know." Charlie could still taste the bitter Amber flavor that even two Rice Krispies Treats couldn't take away. "I was talking to Megan and Claire in chorus. They both went to last year's show and they said she was really good. Really annoying, but really good."

Just then, Mrs. Bauer walked in, wearing her usual ensemble of a long, silky skirt and matching sweater. "Hi, girls," she said, giving them both a warm, perfumed hug. "What's going on? I've spent the whole day writing an article about coping with pets dying, and I need a lift!"

"Ugh," Nicole said. She reached down and gave Dr. Pepper a protective stroke.

"I know," said her mom. "So, tell me, how was school? Did you sign up for the *Robin Hood* auditions?"

"Yep," Nicole said.

"You too?" Her mom turned to Charlie.

Charlie nodded.

"Oh, great! You guys are going to have so much fun. I remember being in those shows in school. We did *The Sound of Music* in high school. That was a good one. I played a nun. . . ."

Suddenly, Nicole's mom stood up, held out her hands, and began to sing. *"Climb every mountain . . ."*

"Mom!" Nicole groaned. *"Please!"*

"Sorry." Her mom laughed. She reached for a Rice Krispies Treat. "I've still got some calls to make. Do you guys need anything before I do?"

"Thanks, Mom, we're okay," Nicole told her. "We're going to go hang out in my room. Look up some songs to sing at our auditions."

"Sounds good," said Mrs. Bauer, turning to smile at Charlie. "Just let me know when you want me to drive you home."

"Thanks, Mrs. Bauer."

"Hey, Mom," called Nicole as her mom walked away. "Remember, this time when we go to Charlie's, we have to take the *long* way."

She winked at Charlie. Past Kyle's house, of course!

Scene 7

The Audition - Act I

That afternoon at Nicole's house was a blast. Almost all of the Amber drama was forgotten as Charlie and Nicole lost themselves in music. Finding a Web site with lyrics was a snap, and by the second song, to their profound amusement, they were inserting "Kyle" into every line they could: *"Oh, what a beautiful Kyle," "Kyle's the one that I want," "Getting to know Kyle . . ."*

Nicole soon zeroed in on a song for herself, but Charlie had a harder time deciding. Something slow? Something upbeat? Just when she'd picked one, another song would come to her that she liked even more.

Finally, she settled on "Tomorrow." Some of the kids might think it was cheesy, but hey — this was a musical! Besides, Nicole swore that when Charlie sang it, it blew her away.

Of course, Charlie and Nicole didn't get around to doing a single minute of homework. But they *did* catch a glimpse of Kyle riding his skateboard as they drove by on the way to Charlie's house. It was, without a doubt, a very good day.

The next day was a different story.

Not only did Charlie have twice as much homework (plus two assignments left over from the day before), but she also had a list of chores from her mom and a little sister who, it seemed, was determined to drive her nuts.

Though Olivia was most complimentary of Charlie's singing, she was sorry to report that it gave Nelson an *awful* headache. No matter where Charlie went to practice, Olivia would follow, politely asking her to stop.

Then Jen and Gwen got home, and suddenly neither singing *nor* homework was an option.

"Could you *please* stop — for one day?" Charlie begged (wondering why Nelson picked on *her* and not her big twin sisters). "It's impossible to concentrate!"

"Do you think it's easy to cheer with you howling upstairs?" Jen said.

"Seriously!" said Gwen. "Ready, Jen?"

"Ready, Gwen! Begin!"

Friday came, and as the day went on, the stomach full of caterpillars Charlie had woken up with turned into a giant swarm of butterflies.

"I can't do it," she moaned, meeting up with Nicole after sixth period. "I didn't get to practice at all last night. I'm going to look like an idiot. I think I'm just going home."

"You are *going* to audition," said Nicole. She grabbed Charlie's arm. "If I have to prop you up and move your mouth for you, you're going to do it. I don't know what you're so *scared* about," she went on, dragging Charlie down the hall. "You sounded great on Wednesday. You're the best singer in our grade. You're gonna be fine!"

Charlie shook her head. "I'm not even sure which song I'm going to sing," she said.

Nicole stopped, at last, outside the auditorium and took Charlie by the shoulders. "Repeat after me," she said. "I, Charlie Moore."

"I, Charlie Moore."

"By the powers vested in me."

"By the powers vested in me."

"Do solemnly swear."

"Do solemnly swear."

"To sing like a superstar."

"To sing like a superstar."

"And show that Amber."

"And show that Amber."

"That sixth graders rule."

"That sixth graders rule."

"AND!" Nicole went on.

"And." Charlie rolled her eyes.

"Increase my Kyle time by five hundred percent."

Charlie smiled. "Okay, let's go."

"After *you,*" said Nicole.

Nicole and Charlie entered the auditorium and walked down the left aisle toward the stage. To Charlie's surprise, the auditorium looked even bigger when it wasn't completely full.

Megan, Claire, Lily, and a bunch of other kids from the sixth grade were already there, along with a lot of seventh and eighth graders, including Amber Wiley. She was turned around — in the first row, of course — in deep discussion with two friends seated behind her, and Charlie couldn't help wondering if she'd told them to sit there so she could have the front row to herself.

As she tilted her head to avoid Amber's gaze,

Charlie felt Nicole give her elbow an eager squeeze.

"On your left, your *left,*" Nicole whispered.

"I know," Charlie mouthed back. As if she, too, hadn't spotted Kyle the minute they'd walked in!

"Hi, Kyle," they said, trying to play it cool as they made their way past his row.

"Hey." He nodded and flashed his usual dreamy grin. "It's cool that you're here."

Then someone called to them from up front. "Hey, guys!" It was Megan, waving and pointing to some empty seats in her row. "Come sit with us!"

"Thanks!" said Nicole. She slid into the first seat and pulled Charlie down beside her.

Up onstage, Mr. Matthews was sitting at the piano, cracking his knuckles. He smiled down at the twittering flock of sixth graders before him and gave them a friendly thumbs-up.

Suddenly, his eyes shifted and refocused on something behind them.

"Hell-oo, hell-oo, hell-*oo!*"

Charlie turned to see a woman approaching, her long black sleeves fluttering in great arcs as she floated down the aisle, flashing a wide-eyed smile over each and every head.

Charlie quickly noticed that everything about the woman was either black (blouse, skirt, tights, shoes, and a tight, shiny bun of hair) or red (lips, cheeks, nails, and scarf — which completely covered the top of her head. In fact, it was tied so tightly that Charlie couldn't help wondering if it held her face in place).

"My, my, *my*!" the woman exclaimed, wafting toward the stage. "What a crowd we have! Well *done,* William! Well *done!*" She swept her arm toward Mr. Matthews as she bounded up the steps. Then she spun around to face the students.

"For those of you who don't know yet," she said, "*I*..." She paused to grab a handful of air and dramatically pull it toward her chest. "... am Lenore Von *Gugenberg.*" She closed her eyes and loudly inhaled the name back in. "But." She opened her eyes wide again. "*Please.* You *must* call me ... *Lenore.*" She lowered her head and gave a deep bow.

Immediately, Nicole elbowed Charlie and silently dared her to laugh. But Lenore's introduction wasn't even the funniest part. Even better was the round of applause that quickly followed from the front row.

"Thank you. *Thank* you," said Lenore, beaming at her biggest fan. "Amber, *darling. Really.* You are *too, too* kind!"

Amber clapped some more, then eagerly raised her hand.

"*Yes?* Please, speak!" Lenore said.

Amber shot up from her seat. "Thank *you!*" she said. Charlie couldn't see her mouth; hearing the words ooze from it was enough. "I just want to say, on behalf of everyone" — she flashed a super-fake grin back over her shoulder at the rest of the kids — "thank *you* so much for doing another show with us! It's just *such* an honor! And *Robin Hood!* Wow! It's a brilliant choice. Really!"

Lenore closed her eyes and nodded, smiling.

"Also," Amber babbled on, "I know I was the star and all last year, and probably will be again this year, but I just wanted to say I know I wouldn't have been half as phenomenal last year if it hadn't been for you."

They shared a rather sickening moment of mutual adoration before Amber continued.

"Anyway, I don't know if you've noticed yet, *Lenore,* but there seem to be an awful lot of, um . . ." She cast a glance over her shoulder again. ". . . sixth graders here. And honestly, I'm not sure it's fair, when most of them won't make the cut, to make us eighth graders and seventh graders sit through *all* these auditions. I mean, I know how *important* this whole process is. But do you think the seventh and eighth graders could all go first, and then the sixth graders—*if* we have time?"

Beside Charlie, Nicole groaned.

"Shhh," Charlie whispered. "Remember, *you're* the reason we're here!"

"Hmm . . ." Lenore stroked her chin with one red nail and considered the idea for a second. Then she turned to Mr. Matthews, who shook his head and frowned.

Lenore turned back to Amber. "*Thank* you for that suggestion, Amber, *darling,*" she said. "But *William* and I have already discussed going in order of the sign-up sheet, as *usual.* And that is how we shall *proceed. But*" — she held up a finger and smiled —"if I am not *mistaken,* that means *you* will be auditioning *first.*"

Amber clapped her hands together eagerly. "I'm ready!" she said.

"*Won*derful," said Lenore. "Then let us *begin*! I trust you've *all* prepared a *song* — mi, mi, mi, *mi-i-i-i* — after which I will ask you to read a *brief* but *telling* monologue. Now! Let's *see. . . .*" She turned and picked up a piece of paper that had been lying on the piano, and slipped on a pair of red glasses hanging from a black chain around her neck. "Let us have the *first* half of this *list* come up on the *stage.* When you are *done,* the *second* half will do the *same.*"

She silently scrolled down the list, then peered out over her glasses.

"As I call your names, listen *care*fully. It *is,*" she said, her eyes widening even more, "the *first* rule of the *stage. Am*ber *Wy*lie. Bellamy *Rich*ards. Marshall Mon*tone . . .*"

Lenore called out each name as if she were announcing that year's Academy Award nominees. Amber and several of her friends were the first bunch called, followed by some other eighth graders, then Megan, Claire, Lily, and Arden. Finally, Lenore called out Nicole's name . . . and stopped.

"*Those* of you whose *names* I've called, *please* line up *quickly* at the back of the *stage*. If I *haven't* called your name, *please* — and *this* is the *second* rule of the *stage* — sit *quietly* in your *seat.*"

Charlie looked at Nicole, her bottom lip working itself into a pout. Separated already! This was not a good way to start.

"Good luck," she mouthed.

Then she watched Nicole and most of her other friends follow Amber onto the stage.

"I know it's not customary," Amber announced as she strode over to the piano and dropped a thin blue folder into Mr. Matthews' hand, "but I've taken the liberty of putting together a medley of songs for *my* audition." She turned to beam at Lenore, who nodded appreciatively in return.

"Oh, *Amber*," she said. "What a *treat!*"

Oh, brother, thought Charlie. *What am I doing here?*

"This looks very . . . interesting," said Mr. Matthews, opening the folder and flipping through the pages.

"Well, I can't *wait* to hear it, Amber. *Please,*" Lenore gushed, "*do* begin."

Charlie leaned over the back of the seat in front of her and watched as Amber planted her feet and whipped her hair over her shoulder. Charlie couldn't help noticing Nicole do the same on the stage, behind Amber. She tried not to laugh as Amber began to sing.

"Someone should really tell her not to try so hard. She's going to hurt herself."

Charlie looked over her shoulder. The seat behind her *had* been empty. But not anymore. Now it was filled by a dark-haired boy with a shell necklace and a wide, easy grin.

"Totally," Charlie whispered back. "Though you gotta admit, she's good."

"Ehh." The boy shrugged. "Whatever. You're probably better. I know my sister is."

"Your sister?"

"Yeah, Megan. Sixth grade. Do you know her?"

Charlie nodded.

"She's great. Really nervous, though. So I came to cheer her on."

He came to cheer on his *sister*? Charlie let the foreign concept sink into her brain. Then she looked at the boy a little harder.

"Are you auditioning, too?" she asked.

"Nah." He grinned and shook his head almost bashfully. "Megan's got all the talent. I can't sing at all. Maybe I'll work on the sets, though. I'm kind of into painting."

Charlie nodded again. "Cool," she said. "I'm Charlie, by the way."

"I'm Ian. Nice to —"

Suddenly, Charlie was all too aware of the music stopping. She looked back up at the stage, where Amber was taking a long, deep bow.

"Bra*va*! Bra*va*!" Lenore said, clapping loudly. "Very, *very* strong! *Thank* you, Amber. *Please*. Take a *seat*. Heather *Al*tus will be next. But *first* . . ." She walked up to the front of the stage and peered over her glasses at the auditorium seats.

"Young lady," she said, her tone at once deeper and darker.

Charlie looked up, her mouth dropping open.

"Yes, *you*," Lenore said. "And the young man *behind* you. I will *not* tolerate *rude* behavior in the *theater*. I expect *complete* silence when*ever* an *actor* is per*for*ming. Do you . . . *understand*?"

Charlie gulped and nodded.

"Yes," she and Ian both replied.

"Very *good*." Lenore turned back around. "Heather *Al*tus. *Please*. Begin!"

Charlie glanced over her shoulder as she slunk down in her seat.

"Sorry," Ian mouthed, making a face that made her smile.

Charlie shrugged. It was just the first miserable moment in what she had already figured out would be a torture-filled afternoon.

What had she been thinking?

If only it were a Tuesday or a Thursday, thought Charlie. If only she had to be home making a snack for Nelson and listening to her sisters cheer. Anything but this. She hadn't even auditioned yet, and already she had made a complete fool of herself.

Charlie sank even deeper into her seat, knowing full well that everyone — including Kyle — had witnessed her humiliation. She could only hope that aliens would invade the school, deem musicals illegal, and erase all memories from everybody's brain.

But to her surprise, Charlie found that by the time it was her friends' turn to audition, the future had brightened somewhat. Megan *did* sound awesome — and she got a standing ovation from her brother. By comparison a lot of Amber's friends had sounded only average.

It was fun, too, to listen to the "lines" Lenore gave them to read. *Where* did *she find them?* Charlie wondered.

Of course, there was Amber. "Where is my youth?" she demanded. "Oh, where are my pretty curls?"

"Mamma! Mamma, you're crying, dear, kind, good Mamma!" read Amber's friend Bellamy in a jarring, ominous voice.

"My father died in a madhouse," began Marshall — rather convincingly, too!

At last, Lenore called Nicole up, and Charlie had to laugh. The way she sang "I'm Gonna Wash That Man Right Outta My Hair" was hilarious — and the moves she had thought up to go with it were perfect. Even Lenore smiled and clapped for her at the end! It made Charlie remember why she liked singing so much. It even made her forget about the butterflies in her stomach — for a minute.

But then Lenore stepped back up onto the stage, sign-up sheet in hand.

"And *now*," Lenore announced, "may I *please* have the *second* group up on*stage*. Listen for your *name*. Then line up in that *order*. Quickly. *Please*. Charlie *Moore*. Andrew *Stein*. Daphne *Wong*. Kyle *Mil*ler . . ."

Charlie stood up and took a deep breath.

"Good luck!" Ian whispered from behind her.

As ready as she'd ever be, Charlie walked down the aisle and climbed the steps onto the stage.

Scene 8

The Audition – Act II

Wow, thought Charlie. *So this is what it's like to be on a real stage.* It was kind of cool, really. Kind of . . . fun.

She looked out over the seats and couldn't help grinning. Back in their row, Nicole was waving to her like crazy while Megan was getting a hug from her grinning brother. *Wow,* thought Charlie. She hadn't even known brothers could do that.

At the piano, Mr. Matthews was stretching out his hands.

"Charlie!" he said as if he hadn't already spent an hour with her in chorus that afternoon. "So! What are you going to sing for us today?"

"Charlie?" The voracious voice of Lenore Von Gugenberg suddenly swooped down. "Are *you*

Charlie *Moore*? My *goodness*." She laughed. "Why, I just *assumed* you were a *boy*! Ha ha *ha*!"

Lenore's laughter was echoed, Charlie realized at once, by Amber's.

Charlie bit her lip. "It's short for Charlotte," she explained meekly.

"Hmph." Lenore snorted. "I do not *believe* in nicknames, you know. *Stage* names, *yes. Nick-* names, *no*. If your *name* is *Charlotte,* then I shall *call* you *Charlotte*." She bent her head to peer at Charlie from above her glasses. *"Please*. Begin! And I trust your audience won't be as *rude* to *you* as you were earlier to *them*."

Reluctantly, and *horribly* embarrassed, Charlie handed Mr. Matthews the sheet of music she'd brought with her, and tried her best to return his friendly smile.

He played a few notes of introduction, then segued into the first verse.

Charlie cleared her throat, closed her eyes, and began to sing. *"The sun'll come out . . ."*

The words lilted out, just as they were supposed to, on pure, sweet notes that seemed blissfully unaware of the nervous girl producing them.

If only she'd kept her eyes closed!

But no, she had to open them, to get the full

effect of the "moment." Unfortunately, the moment included Amber Wiley sitting in the front row, making faces and giggling with her friends, and Lenore Von Gugenberg staring so hard at Charlie, Charlie was afraid her eyes would leave a bruise.

Charlie closed her own eyes again. But it was too late. Her whole body went numb — except that she felt like she might throw up. *Where are those aliens with mind-erasers when you need them?* she thought desperately. *"I just stick out my . . . uh . . ."*

She could hear her notes falling flat, making a mess of the poor, helpless song as she muddled her way to the end. Then she ran off the stage, through the big wooden doors, and into the girls' bathroom.

The knock on the stall door was firm and businesslike.

"Charlie? *Charlie!* I know you're in there. I can hear you. Are you okay?"

"No." Charlie sniffed.

"What's wrong?" Nicole demanded.

"What's *wrong*?" Charlie cried. "Me! That's what's wrong. I can't believe I even *auditioned*." She took a deep breath. "I just humiliated myself in front of everyone!"

Nicole sounded impatient. "What are you

talking about?" she said. "You sounded great! So you stumbled a little in the end."

"But I ran off the stage and skipped the whole line read."

"So you skipped the whole line read. Big deal!" Nicole told her. "Your song still sounded better than anyone else's — including Amber's!"

"Oh, please don't say her name!" begged Charlie. "Did you see her laughing at me?"

"What are talking about?" said Nicole. "Everyone thought you were great! *Including* Amber. I was watching her."

Charlie flipped up the stall latch and eased the door open.

"Really?" she said, her face still dangerously red.

"Really," said Nicole. "Wow . . . you look upset."

Charlie grabbed a wad of toilet paper and wiped it across her nose. Then she looked into the mirror.

Ugh!

She bent over the sink and splashed her face with icy water, then looked into the mirror again.

Ugh!

"This is awful," she said to Nicole. "I messed everything up."

"Listen." Nicole reached her arm around Charlie's shoulders and gave her a tight squeeze. "You did not mess up. I mean, did you hear some of those people? You're not giving yourself enough credit. You are the best singer in this whole school!"

Charlie managed a smile.

"Come on," said Nicole, patting her shoulder. "If we hurry back right now, I bet you can still do a line read. Did you hear mine? 'O Romeo, Romeo! Wherefore art thou Romeo?'" Nicole had to giggle. "And we still have to see Kyle's audition!"

Charlie turned and looked at her face in the mirror again.

"I can't," she said. "But you go." Charlie sniffed a little and waved Nicole on.

Nicole shook her head. "I'll stay with you."

"No way. You have to go," Charlie told her. "You have to watch Kyle and tell me all about it."

"You'll come out as soon as you can?" Nicole asked.

Charlie thought for a moment. She could pull herself together. Stand up straight and walk back into that auditorium. Thank Lenore for the audition and show everybody that she was fine. Or . . .

"I don't think so," she told Nicole. "Just come get me when it's over?"

Scene 9
To Act or Not to Act

If there was a bright side to Charlie's audition, it was that it had been on Friday. She didn't have to face anyone from school for the whole weekend, though she did have the pleasure of reliving every moment in her head. This, along with cleaning the bathrooms and trying to study for Monday's math quiz amid her brother's guitar playing, her sisters' cheering, and Olivia's unending conversations with her invisible friend.

And then there was the trip to the mall on Sunday. You'd think a person could go buy some new jeans in peace — but no! Who did she just barely escape running into at the Gap but Amber Wiley, surrounded (of course) by her usual snooty crew.

"Never mind," Charlie told her mom at once. New jeans would have to wait.

All in all, it was a weekend that Charlie was happy to see end.

Monday morning, she was all set to head to homeroom (in her embarrassingly old jeans) to cram for her math quiz. But Nicole would have none of it.

"Come on!" Nicole said, dragging her off toward the stairs. "Lenore said she'd post the cast list this morning. We've gotta go check it out!"

"Why?" groaned Charlie as she moped along behind her friend. "What if my name's not even on it?"

"It will be," Nicole assured her.

"I doubt it," said Charlie. "If I get any role, I'm sure it will be some kind of Merry Man or something. Something that can wait until *after* math."

"Oh, just be quiet," Nicole said as they reached the third floor. "Today's quiz is going to be easy. You always remember everything, so you'll ace it. And don't tell me you don't want to be the first to know what roles you *and* Kyle get to play!"

Charlie bit her lip. Why was Nicole *always* right?

As they rounded the corner, Charlie couldn't help beginning to imagine what the future might bring. Of course she knew she wouldn't get a lead, having skipped half of the audition. But what if she *was* Maid Marian — and Kyle was Robin Hood? What if they had to rehearse together every single day? What if he fell madly in love with her? (What would Sean say?)

She soon discovered, though, that Nicole was wrong about one thing: she and Charlie were *not* going to be the first ones to find out what parts they'd play. There were already a bunch of kids gathered around the list — or, rather, around *Amber,* who, it seemed, was just *born* to play the role of a five-foot-two brick wall.

"Um, excuse me!" said Nicole, walking up behind her. "Could you let some other people see the list?"

"Hmm?" said Amber distractedly as she continued to study the sheet. "Oh, sure. I just wanted to make sure my name was spelled right. Last year, Lenore left out the 'e.' . . . It happens, you know. I should probably change my last name before I become a star." Flipping her hair across her shoulder, she glanced around and scowled. "Oh! Squeaky Locker Girl and her brace-faced friend are here." Her eyes narrowed coyly and zeroed in on Charlie. "That was some audition you gave on Friday — almost."

Amber's words were like an icy wave, freezing

Charlie in place. But they sure heated Nicole up. Nicole took a step forward. "*You* should keep your opinions to yourself," she said, placing her hands on her hips. "And, like I said, you should move so some other people can see the list."

Amber didn't seem impressed. "You mean you guys want to see if you made the show?" She turned to two friends beside her and laughed. "Hey, why don't you tell me your names again, and I'll tell you if you got anything." She turned back to study the list, then flashed one more smile over her shoulder. "*I'm* Maid Marian, of course."

"Thanks," said Nicole, taking another step forward. "But no thanks. We may only be in sixth grade, but we can read."

This comment got an appreciative laugh from everyone but Amber.

"Whatever," she said, flinging her hair and waving her hand. "Knock yourselves out." She stepped away from the list and headed down the hall.

With Amber gone, the crowd was free to scan the list. But Charlie couldn't bear to look. She glanced around the hall instead, briefly counting the tiles on the floor and the walls.

"So," she whispered finally, giving Nicole's back-pack a tug. "Do you see my name?"

"Well, I see Kyle's!" Nicole whispered back.

"He's Robin Hood! I knew it. I mean, he was so good in auditions. He can sing! You should have seen him." Sighing, she scanned the list some more. "Let's see. . . ."

"It's not on there, is it?" Charlie said. She looked down as a few seventh graders walked up to read the list. She hoped they wouldn't recognize her as the girl who flubbed her audition — soon to be the girl who didn't even get a part in the junior high school show.

"Hang on, hang on," said Nicole. "It's here some — wait! There's mine . . . and there's your name!"

"Don't tell me," said Charlie, at once relieved and wary. "I'm a Merry Man, right?"

"Actually," said Nicole, "*I* am. I'm Little John, can you believe it? But you're not a Merry Man."

"I'm not?" said Charlie. She was stunned. "Really? Are you serious?" She stepped up beside Nicole and scanned the list. "Where am I?"

"Right there," said Nicole, pointing. "You're a 'woodland creature.' "

By fourth-period chorus (after probably failing her math quiz), Charlie had made two very important decisions: one, she would start studying a lot harder from now on, since it was clear she wouldn't be making a living as a Broadway star; and two, she would *not* be doing the school musical.

"What?" said Nicole as they reached the chorus room. "You can't leave me all alone. You have to do the show!"

"You won't be all alone," said Charlie. "You'll have a whole band of Merry Men. And Kyle, too. You'll be, like, his best friend! Me? I'd just be up in some tree or something. Chirping, or howling, or whatever 'woodland creatures' do. Tell me Amber Wiley wouldn't *love* that! I'm just not going to give her the satisfaction. Come on — if you were me, you know you'd do the same thing."

Nicole opened her mouth, about to respond, when Mr. Matthews called the class to attention. "Okay, class, take your seats. We have a lot to cover today."

"We'll talk about this later," Nicole warned as they split off into their respective sections.

Charlie slid into her seat and managed a thin smile in response to Megan's wide one.

"Hey!" Megan whispered. "I saw your name on the cast list! I'm a woodland creature, too!"

"Me too!" Claire chimed in.

Charlie shrugged and nodded. She hoped that Mr. Matthews would hurry up and talk some more.

"Well, well! I have to tell you guys," he began,

waving his baton across the classroom, "I was very pleased with the turnout at the auditions on Friday. And so was Ms. Von Gugenberg."

"You mean *Lenore*!" called out a boy from the baritone row.

Mr. Matthews grinned and nodded. "Yes, *Lenore*. Anyway, you guys did me proud. We've never had one hundred percent turnout from the sixth grade chorus before, and it will most certainly be rewarded!"

There was a round of applause and cheers from the class (at least, from everyone but Charlie).

"Hopefully, by now you've all had a chance to go check out the list of roles. We added a few to accommodate all this talent — so, please, if by some strange chance you don't see your name there, let me know."

Mr. Matthews then walked around his desk and tapped his baton on a thick stack of booklets.

"Ms. Von — *Lenore* — has asked me to go ahead and hand out these scripts. Rehearsals will begin tomorrow, so it wouldn't be a bad idea for you to glance over your script tonight. The show isn't very far away and the more familiar you are with your parts, the better. Miss Moore," he said, his baton drifting over to Charlie, "would you please pass these out?"

With a heavy sigh, Charlie pushed herself out of her seat and took the stack of scripts from Mr. Matthews. She was careful not to look at his irritatingly earnest smile, studying the tassels on his shoes instead.

Keeping her head down, she laid the scripts, one by one, in front of each student and tried to think of them as just a bunch of random papers. To Charlie's annoyance, her eyes seemed determined to scan the covers, as if to remind her of what she'd be missing:

ROBIN HOOD
A Musical Adventure!

What she was *really* dying to do was open the script and start reading. But no. No matter how much she wondered what the songs were like and what lines everyone had, the scripts were for the kids in the show — not for her.

Finally, Charlie placed a booklet in front of Claire, then Megan. She returned the one remaining copy — her copy — to Mr. Matthews' desk, then nonchalantly returned to her seat.

"Miss Moore," Mr. Matthews called as the bell rang at the end of class. "Could you stay for a moment, please? I'll give you a note for your fifth-period teacher."

"Uh . . . sure," said Charlie. She looked over at Nicole and shrugged.

She'd sensed Mr. Matthews' Look all period, from the moment she'd put back her script, and she could tell that he was not happy.

Too bad. Charlie wasn't doing the musical, and nothing he could possibly say would ever change her mind. So what if she didn't get extra credit? She did just fine in chorus already.

As they waited for the rest of the class to filter out, Mr. Matthews sat on the edge of his desk and folded his arms.

"Miss Moore," he began as soon as the room was empty, "I couldn't help noticing you didn't keep a script for yourself."

Charlie slowly nodded.

She knew she couldn't face Mr. Matthews' stare, so she focused instead on the mug beside him. I'LL BE BACH! it said in old-fashioned letters, with a picture of a guy in a wig and dark sunglasses. Charlie read the mug again, still not sure she got it.

"May I ask why you didn't take a script?" Mr. Matthews continued.

"I . . . um . . ." Charlie gave up on the mug and

looked Mr. Matthews in the eye. "Because I'm not going to be in the show."

Mr. Matthews' face creased with concern. "Why not, Charlie?"

She shrugged. "I don't belong in the show. I couldn't even make it through the audition. I made a fool of myself. . . ." She bit her lip. "And I don't want to do it again."

"Oh, Charlie." Mr. Matthews tilted his head. "I thought you did a fine job for your first audition. Lenore thought so, too. I mean, everybody gets nervous, especially the first time they're onstage. But you have real talent. Your voice is a gift, and it would be a pity not to share it with the school. This show needs you, Charlie."

A friendly smile passed over his face, and then the Look returned.

This time, Charlie was ready with a Look of her own. "Oh, come on," she said. "The show doesn't need another 'woodland creature.'"

"In fact," said Mr. Matthews, "the show *does*. And you need the experience. Don't think that Lenore and I didn't discuss it. We could have given you a bigger part; your voice could definitely handle it. But we weren't sure *you* could. And of course there was the fact that we never had the pleasure of hearing your line read. We thought it was better to start you out with a background role that wouldn't put too much pressure on you. Then next year . . ." He grinned. "Look out!"

"Really?" said Charlie. She forced herself to look Mr. Matthews in the eye again. *Is he just saying these things to get one hundred percent class participation?* she wondered.

"Really," he said.

Charlie's eyes wandered across his desk, past the mug, to the script still sitting on the corner.

Mr. Matthews picked it up.

"Well?" he said, offering it to her with both hands. "I promise, you won't be sorry."

Charlie looked at the booklet and felt the teeniest, tiniest bits of excitement slowly begin to creep through her. She had to admit, it was nice — *really nice* — to feel needed and important. And even nicer to be told that she had talent!

"Okay," she said, taking a deep breath and plucking the script from Mr. Matthews' hands. "I'll do it."

"Fantastic!" said Mr. Matthews. He scribbled a note for Ms. Patel, Charlie's science teacher, and laid it on the booklet. "So I'll see you tomorrow in class, and tomorrow afternoon at rehearsal!"

Charlie nodded. "See you tomorrow. And . . . thanks a lot, Mr. Matthews."

Charlie left the chorus room feeling like a new person, or maybe like an old one. She almost felt like the person she'd been before the audition. So what if she had a tiny part? Megan and Claire were woodland creatures, too. The show *was* going to be fun.

And there was something else, too. Charlie had been waiting since September to turn some corner in junior high school, to find her place in it all, to stop feeling like some exchange student who was still learning the language.

She was a nobody in this huge new place. Or if anything, she was "Sean's little sister" (which, if you asked her, was even worse than being nobody). So maybe this was the answer. Maybe this was the key to becoming her own person.

And it all would start tomorrow!

Tomorrow? Charlie gasped and stopped dead in her tracks. Tomorrow was . . . *Tuesday*! What was she thinking?

How was she going to go to rehearsals *and* babysit her sister, too?

Scene 10

A Not-So-Perfect Plan

Charlie walked home from school that day with Nicole close by her side.

"Relax," said Nicole. "I don't know why you're so freaked out. I mean, there's got to be a way for you to be in the show. We'll just explain it to your mom, that's all."

"Explain what to my mom?" said Charlie. "That she has to cancel her afternoon classes so I can be a squirrel in the background of some dumb school play?"

"No," said Nicole. "That maybe, for a few weeks, Jen and Gwen or Sean can come home on Tuesdays and Thursdays and watch Olivia or something. Or aren't there after-school programs at the elementary school?"

Charlie rolled her eyes in exasperation. "Don't

think my mom hasn't tried that. But Olivia absolutely refuses. She ran away, remember? It's bad enough that she has to go without Nelson for six hours in school. Come three o'clock, she just can't take it anymore. Seriously," huffed Charlie, "she is so spoiled!"

"Hey! What about Mrs. Chizzola?"

For a long time, until Olivia started school, Charlie's family had had a babysitter. She was an older woman named Mrs. Chizzola, who had very blond hair with very gray roots and loved to wear shirts with her son's company logo on them. Though Charlie always suspected that Olivia was her favorite, Mrs. Chizzola was always happy to help her with her homework or make time for a game of Scrabble. Charlie missed her a lot.

When Olivia started kindergarten, their mom declared Mrs. Chizzola "economically unsustainable." She assigned Jen and Gwen and (to everyone's horror!) Sean to after-school babysitting duties. Now that Charlie was in junior high, the privilege had been extended to her. And now that her sisters were obsessed with cheering and her brother had guitar lessons, Charlie had discovered she was, well, pretty much stuck.

"Not possible," said Charlie. "My mom got Mrs. Chizzola a job at her school's day care center. She loves it there."

"Well, why can't Olivia go to day care, too?"

Charlie rolled her eyes. "Nicole," she groaned. "Seriously, you are not being helpful."

They walked on in silence, kicking their way through ankle-deep leaves, when Nicole suddenly stopped and yanked on Charlie's elbow.

"I've got it!" she said. "What if we go pick Olivia up from school on Tuesdays and Thursdays and bring her back to rehearsals with us? Her school is right next door. She can read or color or whatever first graders do while we rehearse." Her face was the picture of hopeful delusion. "I'm sure we can duck out for a few minutes to pick her up, don't you think? Olivia would be psyched!"

Charlie chewed on her lip. "Well, maybe." Really, it wasn't such a bad idea. Provided that her mom and Olivia and Lenore all went for it.

"That's what we're doing!" said Nicole, pushing Charlie toward her front door. "Don't worry," she assured her. "It'll work out great!"

"Hmm . . . yeah . . ." Charlie sure wasn't going to get her hopes up as high as Nicole's. But it was definitely worth a shot.

Charlie opened the front door and could instantly hear the boring talk radio station her mom liked so much coming from the kitchen.

Unlike on Tuesdays and Thursdays, Charlie's mom was usually home by the time Charlie got out of school the rest of the week. She taught economics, accounting, and something even more boring-sounding called statistics at the community college in town, and her schedule was far from normal. Mondays and Wednesdays, she taught in the morning and again at night. Tuesdays and Thursdays, she taught all afternoon. And once a month, she led a Saturday seminar that took up most of the day.

Charlie left her backpack in the hall and made her way into the kitchen, with Nicole behind her. Her mom was seated at the table, surrounded by books, folders, and big piles of paper.

"Hi, Mom," Charlie said, stopping in the doorway.

Her mom slowly glanced up, her face in a crumpled frown. "Oh, hi, honey," she said, sliding her glasses off her nose. "Hi there, Nicole. What are you two doing home? Is it two thirty already?" Her head swung around to face the clock on the far wall. "Where does the time go?"

Charlie didn't attempt to answer.

Her mom looked down at the pile in front of her. "Midterms," she said. "Can you believe it's that time already?"

Charlie winced as Nicole pinched her arm.

"Uh . . . Mom . . ." Charlie cleared her throat. "Could I, um, ask you a question?"

"Sure," said her mom. "Shoot."

"Well, there's this musical they're doing at school . . . and I tried out . . . and got a part. . . ."

"Charlie!" Her mom looked up, beaming. "That's wonderful!"

"It's a small part," Charlie said quickly. "Nothing, really."

"It's a great part!" Nicole cut in.

Charlie shushed her with a wave.

"Anyway," Charlie went on. "It's a small part, but Mr. Matthews really wants me to do it, and I think it will be fun."

"I'm sure it will," said her mom. "Good for you!"

Charlie glanced once more at Nicole and nibbled on her lip in preparation for her next words. "Here's the thing, Mom. There are going to be rehearsals every day after school."

"Every day . . . ?" Charlie's mom put down her red grading pencil and slowly rubbed her chin. "Gosh, Charlie, I don't see how that's going to work. Who'll be here for Olivia on Tuesdays and Thursdays after school?"

Charlie sighed. She knew it. *Ouch!* Nicole pinched her again.

"Well . . . actually, Mom . . ." Charlie paused to look at the floor while the radio announcer droned on about the weather. "We had this idea."

"A good one!" said Nicole.

Charlie swallowed. "What if we pick Olivia up from school on Tuesdays and Thursdays and bring her back to rehearsals with us? She can do her homework or something until it's time to go home." She gave her mom the best "please, please, please, *please*" look she could possibly muster. "What do you think, Mom?" she said at last.

Charlie's mom worked her brow for a moment . . . then smiled. "Well, it sounds okay to me, I guess." She looked at Charlie. "But you'll have to explain everything to Mr. Matthews, and tell him that if it doesn't work out, you might not be able to keep going to rehearsals. Make sure he understands. Okay?"

"Sure, Mom!" Charlie grinned. Nicole grabbed her hand and squeezed it as the front door suddenly banged open.

"Easy, Nelson! Easy! Hi, Mom! I'm home!"

Charlie's mom lifted her red pencil and pointed it toward the sound.

"You guys had better go tell Olivia about your plan," she said.

Scene 11

Curtains Up

The next day flew by — even conjugating verbs in Spanish was a blur — and before she knew it, Charlie was following Nicole into the auditorium for rehearsal.

Because they wouldn't be singing during this first rehearsal, Mr. Matthews was not there to greet them. But Lenore Von Gugenberg (who seemed to have gone for a black and purple palette that day) was. She waved to the students, welcoming them to the stage.

"Come! *Come!* By all *means,* don't be *shy!*" she declared. "We're all friends in the *theater!* And we'll be starting very soon!"

Kyle was seated on the edge of the stage, talking to another boy Charlie recognized from Sean's band. Though they could have gone up the left steps, she and Nicole veered from their path to go up the right, past Kyle.

Charlie was glad they'd arrived before rehearsal had started. She still had to see if it was okay to bring Olivia back to rehearsal with her.

"Um, Ms. Von Gugenberg . . . ," she began.

"Please," said the drama teacher, whisking off her plum-colored glasses. "Call me *Lenore*."

"Lenore," Charlie repeated obediently.

"Yes, *Charlotte* . . . am I right? So *glad* to have you in the show."

Charlie tried not to make a face at the old-fashioned name she hated, and smiled instead. "Uh, thank you," she said. "I'm glad, too. . . ." Then she took a deep breath. "I was wondering — my little sister's in first grade, and I'm the one who has to watch her every Tuesday and Thursday afternoon. I really want to do this show, but the only way I can come to rehearsals is if I pick her up and bring her back here. Would that be okay?"

Lenore looked thoughtfully at Charlie. "It's Tuesdays and Thursdays *only,* you say?"

"Oh, yes," said Charlie emphatically. "That's all."

"First *grade,* you say?"

Charlie swallowed hard and nodded. "Uh-huh."

Lenore's eyes softened and her thin violet lips stretched into a grin. "But of *course* you may bring your sister, Charlotte!" she said. Her eyes wandered a little dreamily. "Perhaps it will create an interest in the *theater*! Will you need to bring her *today*?"

"Yes," Charlie answered. "She gets out at three. I'll be really fast. I promise."

Lenore looked at her watch. "Well, it's two thirty-five now. What are we waiting for?" She clapped. "*People!* Let us *begin!*"

Lenore began rehearsals with introductions of the actors and their various roles.

Charlie was still a little self-conscious about declaring herself a "creature," particularly in front of Kyle and Amber. But it turned out to be a whole lot easier when she discovered that she shared the forest with not just Megan and Claire but a bunch of other kids from chorus and a cool girl from her math class, too.

It was actually a fine part, as it turned out; there were lots of songs to sing and no lines to memorize. But not so for Nicole! As she and Charlie had discovered the night before when they'd read the script, Nicole had tons of lines, a fact that made her a little nervous. But she also had a lot of very close scenes with Kyle! Sure, she'd be dressed like a Merry Man. But still, she was thrilled.

When introductions were complete, Lenore had the cast circle around, and explained how they'd start rehearsals.

"The *theater*," she began, sweeping her arms out dramatically, "is like any other *craft*. Just as an *artist* must mix her *paints* or a *potter* must knead her *clay,* we *too* must prime our *own* materials.

"Can anyone tell me," she said, scanning her audience, "what these *materials* are?"

Instantly, Amber's hand shot up into the air.

Lenore smiled at her warmly. "*Yes,* Amber. *Do* tell."

Some invisible string suddenly seemed to lift Amber's head higher. "Our body," she said brightly, "and our voice."

Lenore rewarded her efforts with a small round of applause. "Quite right!" She cleared her throat and continued. "I cannot stress *enough* how *vital* it is that we give our bodies and our voices the *utmost* care *and* respect. You *will*," she bellowed, nearly making Charlie jump, "drink *water* — more than you ever have before. You *will* warm up your *voices* and your *bodies,* and *not* just at rehearsals, but each *morning,* as well. And you will *not* be late or" — her hand flew up to her forehead — "oh, the *horror* — absent!

"Have I made myself *clear*? Very *good.* Then let's

begin our warm-ups, *shall* we? Heads *up*. Feet *firmly* beneath you. Shoulders *back . . . hmm . . .*" One side of Lenore's lip rose in a dubious purple sneer. "Perhaps we need a demonstra —"

Amber's hand was already in the air.

"Why, *thank* you, Amber."

Amber stepped up beside Lenore and modeled the proper dramatic warm-up "stance." (Her smug expression was, Charlie assumed, purely optional.) She then led them in a brisk series of head rolls, arm circles, waist bends, and hand and foot shakes — kind of like the hokey pokey, but much more dramatic!

These physical warm-ups were followed by vocal ones, which required a partner. Charlie and Nicole quickly found each other, then watched, annoyed, as Amber claimed Kyle as her own.

"Now," explained Lenore, "I want you to watch each other's faces *carefully* — really see how they *work* — as you take a deep breath *in . . .* and let it *out. Hummm . . . slowly* opening your mouths . . . *ahhhh . . .* from the diaphragm now . . . that's it. . . ."

"AHHHHH!"

Charlie and Nicole both spun around. What was *that*?

"Amber, *dear,*" said Lenore, "*remember,* this is

not a *performance*. There's no need to warm up so *loudly*."

Nicole snickered. "That came from a lot more than her diaphragm!" she whispered.

At last, after they had practiced their "e-NUN-see-AY-tion" by saying "U*nique* New *York*" back and forth with their partners, Lenore glanced at her watch and clapped her hands together smartly.

"All right then, let's take *five,* shall we?" she said. She smiled and nodded at Charlie. "When we *resume,* we'll do a first run-through of *lines* as our characters! *Go!* Drink *water!*"

Without even grabbing her jacket, Charlie dashed outside and across the field to Olivia's school. Olivia's first grade class was just dismissing, and Olivia smiled when she saw Charlie running up to her line.

"Charlie!" said Mrs. Roach, who had been her first grade teacher, too. (She was much nicer — and prettier — than her unfortunate name suggested.)

Charlie gave her a hug.

"So, I hear you're taking Olivia back to Roosevelt with you."

Charlie sighed and nodded as she reached for Olivia's hand.

"She's very excited," Mrs. Roach told her, with one of her teacherly nods.

Charlie looked down at Olivia, who was grinning widely. *Hmmm,* thought Charlie. Olivia sure hadn't seemed so excited the night before when Charlie had told her what the plan was. She'd run away in tears! Of course, that could have been the result of the threats Charlie made to Nelson if Olivia embarrassed her in any way. . . .

"Nice to see you, Mrs. Roach," Charlie said. "We've got to run, I'm afraid! Bye!"

Charlie hurried back to school, dragging Olivia beside her. She had already primed herself to nag and threaten and basically do whatever it took to make Olivia keep up. To her surprise, however, Olivia seemed to be doing the best she could.

She skipped up to the front door of the junior high behind Charlie, at which point Charlie spun around and gripped her by the shoulders.

"Okay," she said, working to catch her breath. "I know you can't understand this, but this is *very* important. This is junior high school, not elementary school. People have *reputations* to think about in junior high school." She stared gravely into her little sister's eyes. "Do you have any idea what I'm saying?"

Olivia knit her brow very seriously and nodded.

"You do?" said Charlie. "Really?"

"Yeah," said her sister, still nodding. Then she

glanced over her shoulder. "Nelson knows all about junior high. He watches you sometimes, too." She grinned, then offered up her ear. "Oh! That's so nice! Nelson says if you don't have any friends here, that's okay. He'll be your friend."

"Ugh!" Charlie groaned, deflated, and hung her head. She checked her watch — she didn't have time for this! — and opened the door.

Towing her sister behind her, Charlie slipped into the auditorium. She plopped Olivia down in a seat in the very last row. Onstage, Lenore was already gathering everyone together.

"Just sit here and be very, very quiet, okay?" Charlie begged. "I don't know how long this will take today, but if you *promise* not to bother me, I'll . . . I'll . . . oh, I don't know . . ."

"Give me money for ice cream tomorrow?" Olivia suggested.

"Yeah, sure."

Olivia smiled and nodded. "I promise."

It wasn't until the cast had finished their line read that Charlie realized that Olivia hadn't bothered her at all.

She whipped her head around and scoured the seats, back to front, and front to back again, searching for her sister's tight blond curls.

Charlie suddenly felt sick. She didn't see Olivia anywhere! *Oh, no!* Charlie's heart pounded wildly. *What have I done?*

She was just about to jump off the stage to see if maybe, just maybe, Olivia was on the floor behind the seats when the tinkly sound of her sister's laughter wafted to her from the wings of the stage. Charlie turned and stomped off toward it.

"Olivia!" she said, spotting her sister. Charlie was still numb but also furious. "I thought I told you to stay put!"

Olivia, who was seated cross-legged on the dusty floor, looked up innocently. Only then did Charlie notice that Olivia wasn't alone. Beside her was a tall boy she knew she'd seen before — Megan's brother, Ian. In his lap was a big sketch pad; on his face, a friendly smile.

"Hi," he said. "Is this your sister?"

Charlie stood speechless, way too shaken to be polite.

"Oh, hey, I'm really sorry," Ian said, pulling himself up. He laid the pad down next to Olivia and dusted his jeans off. "Did you wonder where she was? You know, I saw her down there"— he nodded offstage —"when I came in to meet about sets, and she just looked so bored, I thought I'd try to entertain her." He grinned apologetically.

"He's a really good drawer!" Olivia piped up. "Here! Look!" She handed the sketch pad up to Charlie.

The drawing on the top was really, *really* good, though Charlie wasn't *exactly* sure what it was supposed to be of. It was a figure — a cute one — some kind of monkeyish, bearish, alien sort of creature, with great big ears, a furry Mohawk, and a small polka-dot tie.

"It's Nelson!" said Olivia proudly, reaching up to take the pad back.

"We were talking, you know, but I was having a hard time seeing him," Ian explained matter-of-factly. "So I asked her to describe him." He smiled at Charlie and winked.

Charlie looked down at the drawing. *So that's what Nelson looks like.* She handed the pad back to her sister, then looked at Ian and — she couldn't help it — smiled.

"You're a really good artist," she told him.

He grinned and shrugged. "Thanks. Oh, and hey." He glanced back up at her. "You're a really good singer, you know. Your audition was great. What part did you get, anyway?"

Charlie rolled her eyes. "A squirrel."

"Cool!" said Ian, nodding. "Megan's a raccoon. That's awesome."

It was Charlie's turn to shrug. "I guess so," she said. Then she took a deep breath and looked back at her sister. "I hope she wasn't too much of a pest," she said to Ian.

"Her? No way! She's a riot! She says you're going to bring her every Tuesday and Thursday. Is that true? And she said if she didn't have any homework, she'd help me with the sets. Didn't you, Olivia?"

Olivia's face lit up in a two-front-toothless smile as she eagerly nodded. "Yeah!" she chirped back.

"Oh." Charlie shook her head. "You don't have to do that. Really."

"No, no, it's no problem," Ian assured her. "It'll be great. We need the help. She's done a lot already." He nodded at some sketches of backgrounds on the wall. "That tree with the big knothole, that was her idea."

"And Nelson's!" Olivia piped up.

"And Nelson's." Ian smiled again, and Charlie had to smile, too.

Scene 12

Lines, Lines, Lines!

Weeks passed, and to Charlie's relief, having Olivia come to rehearsals with her was the easiest thing in the world. Ian kept her totally busy, painting or papier-mâchéing or gluing leaves on cardboard trees. And when he didn't have something for her to do, Lenore came through, asking Olivia to fetch her water or hunt for her glasses if they ever *mysteriously* disappeared.

"How *charming*!" she'd say, smiling and patting Olivia on the head. "And what an *imagination*!"

Olivia was in heaven, and Charlie was pretty content, too. She'd been disappointed at first to have such a small role, but it sure took the pressure off! Except for the fact that Nicole's role put her closer to Kyle, Charlie wasn't jealous of her friend's bigger part at all.

While Nicole had to run through her scenes *over* and *over,* Charlie could basically sit back, sing with her friends, do a little homework if she needed to, and enjoy the show. (Who wouldn't love seeing Nicole and the Merry Men try to learn a dance number?) She and Megan made up funny lines to one of their woodland songs — and then had to remember not to sing them in front of Lenore! But Nicole was feeling the pressure.

"Why did I let you talk me into this?" she moaned to Charlie one Friday night as they were hanging out in her room. She'd invited Charlie to sleep over and help her with her lines.

Charlie rolled over on her friend's enormous canopy bed. "Me!" she said. She laughed as Nicole let out a dramatic sigh.

"I'm sorry!" said Nicole. "But can you blame me? I mean, how am I supposed to concentrate on a stage with Kyle? It's not humanly possible."

"Well," said Charlie coyly, "Amber seems to do it."

"Amber! *Ugh!* Don't get me started!" Nicole jumped down and posed before her full-length mirror. "I mean, did you hear what she said to me at that costume fitting today?" Nicole put her hands on her hips and flipped her head in a dead-on Amber impersonation. "'Better make sure your costume isn't *green* or everyone will think you're the Jolly Green Giant.' Right in front of Kyle! *Oooh,* she makes me so mad!"

"Well, did you hear what she said to me?" Charlie flipped her own hair and stuck her chin out. "'Too bad you're not a rabbit. With those ears, you wouldn't even need a costume.'" Charlie wrinkled her lip.

"What do people *see* in her?" Nicole asked.

"I don't know," said Charlie. And she really didn't. For absolutely no reason she could think of, Amber Wiley seemed to have a huge bunch of eighth grade friends. She wasn't even nice to them! And if she *was* nice to them, it was clearly because she wanted something. There was one exception, of course: Kyle.

"Well, enough about her!" declared Nicole. She grabbed a crumpled script from her desk and plopped down onto her bed next to Charlie. "I mean, we have some serious work to do here! You have to help me get this second act down."

Without missing a beat or looking at her script, Charlie broke into the opening line of the second act's first scene: "What, ho! Who have we here, pray tell?"

Nicole looked at her, a little surprised, then

checked her script for her own line. "Aye, Robin."
She cleared her throat and tried to bring her voice
down a few octaves. "Aye, Robin, 'tis —"

But before she could go on, the door to Nicole's
room swung open and her mom peeked in.

"'Tis I!" she said brightly, "bearing a platter of
refreshment, if it please you, m'ladies." She stepped
in carrying a tray with a real teapot, teacups with
saucers, and a plate full of oatmeal cookies. "Tea,
anyone? I'll pour."

"Sure!" said Charlie as Nicole's mom set the tray
on the desk.

"It's lemon zinger, with honey," she said as she
filled a cup for Charlie. "Good for the throat,
you know."

Hmmm, Charlie thought as she took a bite of
chewy cookie. *I wonder if fresh-baked cookies and
room service ever get old . . . ?*

"So," Nicole's mom said after the tea was poured
and served. "Opening night's not too far away!"

"Don't remind us, Mom," groaned Nicole.

"Oh, come on!" Mrs. Bauer replied. "You are
going to be great! I'm so proud of you both! And
guess what, Nicole? I forgot to tell you. Your great-
aunt Velva said she would come to the show with
Grandma Mary and Grandpa Frank! Won't that
be fun?"

Nicole rolled her eyes. "Mom," she groaned. "I mean, how many does that make now? Plus you and Dad and the mailman! I don't even think they'll let one kid bring that many people."

"Oh, don't be silly! When I was in school plays, I always had the first two rows filled, at least, and nobody complained!" She winked at the girls and moved to the door. "Call if you need anything. Okay?"

Nicole shooed her mom away, looking relieved to see her go, then took a sip of tea.

"So, which show is your mom coming to?" she asked Charlie. "My parents are so crazy, they're coming to both."

Charlie reached for another cookie and took a bite before she spoke. This wasn't a happy subject at all.

"I don't think my mom's coming to any," said Charlie flatly.

"What do you mean?" said Nicole.

Charlie shrugged. "I've reminded her, I've put flyers on the refrigerator, I walk around the house singing until Sean pulls my hair to make me stop, and still, there's nothing written on her calendar. Nothing."

"So?" said Nicole. "I'm still sure she's planning on going."

Charlie shook her head. Nicole was so naïve. "You know my mom. If she doesn't write it down, it isn't happening. And I shouldn't have to remind her!" After all, her mom had all of the twins' games, Sean's guitar lessons, and Olivia's playdates written down. Charlie was sick of being forgotten!

"So don't worry about having enough seats for your whole family," Charlie went on. "They can have mine." She let Dr. Pepper slink into her lap, and softly rubbed his chin.

"You don't think Sean or your sisters will come?"

Charlie made a face. "Are you crazy? If it's not a football game, no way will Jen or Gwen be there. And Sean? He couldn't care less." She scratched between the cat's ears. "Olivia will come with me, I guess . . . and, of course, Nelson will need his own seat."

She looked at Nicole and they laughed.

"Hey, speaking of Olivia, who is that guy she's always helping? I mean, am I wrong, or is he kind of cute?"

"Who, Ian?" asked Charlie. Cute? Well, yeah . . . she guessed he *was* kind of cute.

"How do you know him?" asked Nicole.

Charlie shrugged. "He's Megan's brother. He's in seventh grade."

"And he's working on the sets?"

Charlie nodded. "He's a really good artist. And he's great with kids — thank goodness!" Charlie smiled without even thinking. "He's really nice to talk to."

Nicole seemed to file the information away in her brain. "Cool," she said. "Hey, we'd better get back to work." She put down her cup and reached for her script. Then, after hesitating for a moment, she offered the script to Charlie.

"I guess it's probably better if I don't read this thing. You want it?"

"Nah," Charlie said. Somehow, she'd realized, she'd memorized almost the whole play already. She wasn't sure how. She certainly hadn't tried to. But just like the poems in English class, she found, it was there.

"Let's just do it. Ready, Little John? 'What, ho! Who have we here . . .'"

Scene 13

The Squirrel Takes the Stage

The next Monday, Charlie floated to rehearsals, borne on a cloud of 100 percent correct answers on her math quiz. What a way to start the week!

She was still glowing when Lenore clapped her hands and called the group to attention.

"Good *afternoon,* cast. What a day! What a *day!*" Her smile was blinding. "Is everyone *here*? Let's begin!"

She led them in the usual warm-up of facial contortions and unnatural sounds, which Charlie still couldn't help giggling through, then declared that for this rehearsal they'd be focusing on Act Two.

Nicole squeezed Charlie's arm. "Am I glad you helped me with that!" she whispered.

"Woodland creatures," said Lenore. "I need you

in the trees." She pointed upstage with a long, fuchsia-nailed finger.

"Do you mean the ladders?" Arden, who was playing a woodpecker, asked.

Lenore inhaled deeply and deliberately through her nose. *"No,"* she said, pushing the air out with the word. "I *mean* the *trees.*"

"Oh . . . right," said Arden.

"Robin Hood, you'll be *here,* at center stage. Little John, *please,* take your mark here on his left."

Nicole squeezed Charlie's arm once more, then skipped off to take her place next to Kyle. Charlie, meanwhile, felt the warm glow of her math quiz victory slowly fade as she climbed, most unsquirrel-like, into her "branch" in the "tree." "Ouch! Hey!" She snatched her hand out from under the enormous feet of the owl, Alex. "You stepped on my paw!"

"Merry Men, stage left. And Maid Marian and her ladies-in-waiting, you should be awaiting your *cue* off stage right. Hurry now!" Lenore's hands fluttered in a million different directions. "And if you're not in the scene, *please,* remove yourselves from the stage. Mr. Matthews, some opening *music,* if you *please.*"

"Uh, Lenore?" Suddenly, Bellamy, an eighth

grade lady-in-waiting, raised her hand. "Amber — I mean, Maid Marian" — from day one, Lenore had insisted they *be* their characters at all times — "isn't, um, here."

Lenore recoiled, wide-eyed, in horror. "Not *here*? What? Is she *ill*?"

Bellamy shook her head and shrugged. "She was in school today."

Lenore's forehead creased and her inky, arched eyebrows met darkly. On the floor, her jazz shoe tapped hard once, twice, three times, then stopped in midair. "Well, I don't know *what* she could be doing that is more important than *this,* but I *do* know that the *show* must go *on!* If a character isn't here, then we'll just have to use a *stand-in.* Now . . ." She smoothed her scarf as if trying to soothe her shaken nerves. "The question is, *who*?"

Charlie looked down, sorry to see Lenore's mood change but greatly enjoying the certain misery it meant for Amber! Then, all of a sudden, she noticed Nicole stepping forward.

"*Yes,* Little John?"

"Well, I think you should let Charlie — I mean, Charlotte — er, the squirrel — do it."

Lenore glanced into the tree where Charlie was precariously perched, then quickly turned back to Nicole. "The *squirrel*?"

"Yes, the squirrel." Nicole nodded eagerly while Charlie's eyes widened in panic. "She knows all the lines. Really!"

Lenore turned and moved to the foot of Charlie's tree. "Is this *true*?" she asked, pointing her finger up at Charlie like a hunter stalking his prey. Charlie suddenly felt more in touch with her character than she ever had before.

"Uh . . . well . . . I don't know if I know them *all* . . ."

But there was no defending herself against *this* hunter.

"Get down from there this *instant*. Prepare yourself. Today, you are Maid *Marian*. Places, everyone. Let's *begin!*"

With every eye in the auditorium on her, Charlie descended from her perch and took her place in the wings. As she passed Mr. Matthews, he smiled at her broadly, giving her a big thumbs-up and an encouraging nod. This was quickly offset, however, by the pair of icy stares bestowed by Marian's faithful ladies-in-waiting — Bellamy and Amber's other cohort, Jenna.

Charlie gulped, turned to the stage, and glared at Nicole.

But when Lenore said, "Begin!" and the music started, everything changed. Suddenly, Charlie wasn't a scared, self-conscious sixth grader any longer. She was a noble lady, the charge of King Richard, clever and full of charm.

It was amazing—a whole different experience than her audition. Maybe it was because she'd watched the rehearsals so many times. Maybe it was because there were other people on the stage with her. Maybe it was because Amber wasn't there laughing at her. But Charlie wasn't nervous at all. How speaking these crazy lines and singing a duet with Kyle could feel natural, she didn't know. But it did.

Before she knew it, Kyle was reaching for her hand, sweetly looking into her blue eyes, and —

"Sorry I'm late, everyone. *Hey!*"

Amber charged at the stage with a big box in her hands and a crazed look in her eyes. "What's going on here?"

Lenore strode from her place near the wings to meet Amber. "What's going on, *indeed*," she said, pursing her brightly colored lips sternly. "*Really,* Amber. I expected *much* more from you. You know very *well* that the *theater* does not wait. You're *very* late. It's *utterly* unacceptable." She paused for a moment to allow her chin to tremble. "Particularly *today,* of all days."

"Bu —" Amber stood there, wide-mouthed and

frozen, then finally blurted, "But it's not my fault! My locker was stuck. I had to ask the janitor to get it open."

Lenore simply, but very *dramatically,* rolled her eyes in response. "Your *locker,*" she said dryly, "could have waited until *after* rehearsal."

"You're absolutely right, Lenore." Amber nodded, composed again. "And I apologize profusely. I guess I was just so determined to get *this* and bring it to you."

With that, Amber lifted the box she'd been carrying and placed it on the stage. Then she pulled off a strip of tape and raised the lid.

Charlie and most of the cast scootched forward to peer into the box. Inside, Charlie could just barely make out something white, with what looked like two faces, one sad and one happy, drawn in pink.

"Happy birthday!" Amber sang out, beaming at Lenore proudly.

Lenore's hands flew to her mouth, where they clapped several times with girlish pleasure. "Oh! Is that . . . for *me*?" she gasped. "Why, Amber, *darling.* How *ever* did you know?"

"Oh, I have my ways!" Amber said. "Do you like it? I wanted to surprise you. I made it myself. With the comedy/tragedy symbol and everything."

"Indeed!" gushed Lenore. "The two sides of

Dionysus, the god of Greek *theater*! An inspiration to us *all*! It's wonderful. *Simply* wonderful!" She clutched her hands tightly in glee.

Amber smiled smugly and shifted her eyes, ever so briefly, to flash Charlie a frigid glare. "I'm glad you like it," she said, focusing on Lenore once again. "I'm just so very, very sorry I was late."

"Oh!" Lenore waved the ridiculous words away. "Don't be *silly*. Besides"— she offered her hand to help Amber onto the stage —"it's really the others whom I am *most* concerned about in this scene. Come. The important thing is you're here now. Shall we go through the scene again, from the top?" She glanced down at the cake, which was smiling and frowning appetizingly from its box. "Or perhaps"— she bit her lip —"we should take five!"

After singing a chorus of "Happy Birthday" and choking down a piece of Amber's (disappointingly tasty) cake, Charlie was back to her tree, and just like after midnight in a fairy tale, all was as it had been before.

"Ow! Alex, watch it! Seriously!"

But like Cinderella, she'd always have the memories. Acting with Kyle, the surprising thrill of working the stage and being at the center of it all, and, of course, the look on Amber's face when she came in! The image kept a smile on Charlie's squirrel face for the rest of the rehearsal.

"Great job today," said Mr. Matthews, walking up to Charlie when rehearsal finished.

"Oh, thanks," said Charlie.

"I knew you could sing, but you have a real thing for learning lines."

Charlie shrugged and felt her cheeks flush.

"You do, *indeed.*" Charlie started at the feel of a shockingly cool hand on her shoulder. She looked up to see Lenore standing beside her, smiling. "Your talents were *most* appreciated today, *Charlotte,* my dear. Oh!" Her eyes wandered into the distance. "Pardon me. I *must* go thank Amber again."

"Happy birthday," Charlie and Mr. Matthews called as they watched her go. Mr. Matthews chuckled.

"Well, I'd better go, too," he said, slipping his sheet music into an old briefcase. "I just wanted you to know that I'm really glad you're here. See you tomorrow!"

"See you." Charlie smiled. Then she skipped off the stage, eager to find Nicole. Whether she'd say "How could you?" or "Thanks!" when she found her was still to be determined.

When Charlie got to the seats where she and Nicole had left their backpacks, Nicole's blue bag was there, but she wasn't. Ian, however, was.

"Hi," he said, hoisting his own bag onto his shoulder. "You were awesome today." He smiled. "I just had to tell you. Seriously, when you started singing, the whole stage crew got up to watch."

Charlie stood there, truly stunned. She opened her mouth to respond — but didn't have the slightest idea what to say.

"So, yeah . . . ," Ian went on. Her lack of words, it seemed, was contagious. "I . . . uh . . . yeah. So, I just wanted to say that . . . and . . . um . . ."

"Charlie!"

Charlie turned to see Nicole walking down the aisle — with Kyle! She was clearly trying to play it cool, but her eyes screamed, *Check it out!*

"He was looking for you," she said, running up and squeezing Charlie's forearm *really* hard. "Weren't you, Kyle?" She turned to him, then back to Charlie, then back to Kyle again.

"Uh . . . hi, Kyle," said Charlie as Ian's surprising compliments faded in the wake of this new and way more unexpected guest.

Kyle flashed his perfect white teeth. "Hey." He nodded to Ian and turned to Charlie again. "It's raining. My mom's here. Do you need a ride?"

Charlie suddenly wondered if maybe she was in a fairy tale after all. Where had this unbelievable day come from?

"M-me? Really?" she stammered, half stunned and half distracted by the frantic gestures Nicole was making behind Kyle's back. "I mean, sure."

"Great." Kyle kept smiling and turned to Nicole. "I already asked Nicole, but it sounds like she's all set."

Suddenly, Nicole looked like the sad half of Lenore's birthday cake. "Yeah, I have to go to the orthodontist. My mom is probably here already."

Kyle shrugged. "Too bad. Next time?" he said.

"Next time?" said Nicole. "Sure!"

"So." Kyle turned back to Charlie. "Ready?"

Charlie nodded and grabbed her bag, then locked eyes with Nicole. "Bye," she squeaked. "Oh . . . and bye, Ian. Thanks again."

The rain was pounding, and even though she'd trudged through worse before, Charlie closed her eyes in silent thanks for having a dry ride home. Not to mention who that ride was with!

Kyle's mom was waiting in their minivan just outside the entrance. Still, the dash from door to door left Charlie dripping.

"Hey, Mom," said Kyle as he climbed in

after Charlie and slid the door shut. "Mind taking Charlie home?"

As Charlie scooted across the backseat, Kyle's mom spun around to flash a smile as bright and charming as her son's. Her hair, Charlie noted, was impeccably styled, and her workout clothes were white and spotless. *Does she really go to the gym like that?* Charlie couldn't help wondering. *And if she does go to the gym, does she sweat at all?*

"Why, hi there, Charlie!" Kyle's mom said. "It's great to see you. My, my! Are you at *Roosevelt* now? How do you like it?" She shook her head before Charlie could answer and sighed. "Goodness, how the time flies. Honestly, I still think of you as a baby! Where *do* the years go?"

By now, Charlie had remembered that Kyle's mom's questions, like her own mom's, seldom required answers, so she focused instead on trying to look as *un*babyish as she could.

She snuck a peek in Kyle's direction. *Too late,* she thought. Kyle was staring out the window, probably picturing her in diapers. Great. She felt sick.

Still shaking her head, Kyle's mom started the engine.

"So, are you in the musical, too, Charlie?"

The silence that followed made Charlie look up, at last, and wonder if maybe she should answer.

But just as her lips moved to form a reply, Kyle's mom started talking again.

"Kyle's loving it. Aren't you, Kyle? Robin Hood! Can you believe it? He's loved that story since he was little. Haven't you, Kyle? Have you kids gotten your costumes yet? Remember that little costume you had when you were three? What happened to that? . . . Oh, look! Here we are. This is your house, isn't it, Charlie?"

The van turned gently into Charlie's driveway and stopped.

So. That was it. The ride was over. Charlie didn't know what she'd expected to happen . . . but she did know it hadn't happened. Nothing. Or, as Señora Greenberg said in Spanish class, *"Nada."*

"Uh, thanks, Mrs. Miller," she said, glancing quickly at Kyle, who was already sliding the door open. He smiled at her and, suddenly, everything seemed right again.

"Say hi to Sean," he said, smiling. "Tell him I'll come by later."

Charlie nodded. "Okay."

"And say hi to Gwen and Jen."

"Okay."

"And . . . uh . . . your friend Nicole, too, if you talk to her."

Charlie swallowed. "I will."

"This *is* your house, isn't it?" Kyle's mom spoke up at last from the front seat. And suddenly Charlie noticed how much rain she was letting in. Quickly, she slipped out, dragging her backpack, and tugged the car door shut behind her.

"He totally likes you!" Nicole said on the phone ten minutes later.

"Likes me?" said Charlie. Nicole might as well have said the Queen of England wanted Charlie to take over her throne. It would have been just as likely. Charlie couldn't help smiling, though. "He didn't say much in the car, you know."

"Oh, that just means he likes you even *more*! Trust me. He gave you a ride home. Why did I have to go to the stupid orthodontist today and miss it? Oh, but listen to this." Nicole's juicy gossip voice suddenly kicked in. "You should have seen the look on Amber's face when you walked out with Kyle. Priceless! I mean, she was out-of-her-mind jealous."

"Really?" said Charlie. Amber? Jealous of *her*? The universe really had turned upside down!

"Oh yeah. I'm telling you," said Nicole, "Kyle likes you — and Amber knows it!"

Scene 14
Worst Day Ever

It was a very good thing that Charlie had such a great day on Monday, because everything went downhill on Tuesday.

It started with her English test, which was not as easy as she'd hoped. And then there was science, where her lab experiment exploded when it should have just changed color.

"That's why we wear goggles," said her teacher, Ms. Patel. "Too bad we don't wear lab coats, too. I doubt that's going to come out of your sweater."

Then there was rehearsal, where junior high school truly reached an all-time low.

From the minute she walked into the auditorium, Charlie knew there would be trouble. Clearly, word had gone out: every single eighth grade girl in the show was to make Charlie's life as miserable as possible.

It started with mere snickering and a good amount of pointing. That, Charlie could have handled. After all, it had happened now and then at rehearsals — whenever Amber was bored. But the torture didn't stop there. One by one, the older girls would walk by her, commenting on her hair ("Do you even *wash* it?"), or her clothes ("What's that huge spot on your sweater? Your *lunch*?"), or her family ("Who's the weirdest? You or your little sister?"). She prayed that Kyle wouldn't overhear any of the nasty comments. But there was no reason to worry. Amber made sure to keep him as far from Charlie as possible.

After a warm-up filled with vicious stares from Amber and her crew, Charlie was actually relieved to go pick Olivia up from school. But that relief was short-lived. No sooner had they returned than Olivia was dancing up in front of Kyle with a big goofy grin across her freckled face.

"Hey." Kyle nodded down at Olivia, turning away from Amber. He glanced up at Charlie, whose stomach was tied in knots, and winked.

But before Charlie could say anything, Olivia spoke up.

"Guess what?" Olivia chirped.

"What?" Kyle said.

Olivia hopped from foot to foot, pretty much looking like her news was that she had to pee. Then, finally, she spoke.

"My sister likes you!" Olivia hunched her shoulders gleefully, then spun around and began to sing: "Charlie and Kyle, sitting in a tree, K-I-S-S-I-N-G. First comes love. Then comes —"

Somewhere inside Charlie, some basic survival instinct was activated. She grabbed Olivia by the backpack and dragged her, still singing, out the door and into the hall.

"What?" whined Olivia, as if Charlie had mortally embarrassed *her* or something. "That's what you said on the phone last night."

Charlie's face was so hot she thought her headband would melt. "You were listening to my conversation?"

Olivia shrugged. "Nelson and I always do. It's the only way to learn stuff."

Charlie looked down at her sister's perfectly unapologetic face, wanting at once to scream and cry and disappear forever . . . and ever.

And then the door opened.

"Hey, Charlie. We're starting. The sets are up and everything." There were Megan and Claire. "Oh, and, Olivia, Lenore wants you."

Seizing the opportunity, Olivia wiggled away from Charlie and dashed between the two girls. "Coming!" she called.

Megan stood back and watched her go, then turned to study Charlie. "Is . . . something wrong?" she asked.

Charlie shook her head. "Try *everything*," she moaned. "Amber hates my guts, and my sister just told Kyle I liked him. And if there's anything else I'm forgetting, please *don't* let me know."

Megan looked at Claire. "You like Kyle?" she said.

Charlie nodded. Didn't everyone?

"Well, don't worry," said Claire, trying to sound cheerful. "She's just a little kid. No one listens to them."

"Totally," said Megan. "And who cares about Amber? She acts like this is her own personal show. I will be *so* happy next year when she's in high school."

"Definitely," said Claire. "You know, we've got to stick together, not let them think they can get away with treating us like babies."

"Or like we don't matter," agreed Megan.

But Charlie just sighed. "I don't know," she said. "It's fun to be in a musical and all, but it's not fun to deal with them. I should just forget about this year, and try again next year."

"What are you talking about?" said Claire. "You've been rehearsing for weeks — and we need you!"

"Yeah," said Megan. "Without you, we won't be half as good."

"And who's going to remind the leads of all the lines they miss?" Claire went on. "How do you do that, anyway? Plus, you have to see the trees they've put up for us. They're really cute!" She grinned proudly.

"Really?" Charlie said. She'd seen Olivia helping Ian with the trees, and she could tell they were pretty cool.

"Yeah," said Megan proudly. "They were all my brother's idea." Then her face got a little more serious. "Also, I may be wrong, but if you quit on Lenore this time, she just might not let you be in the show next year."

Charlie thought about this for a moment. Megan probably had a point. Dropping out now could ruin Charlie's musical hopes forever. She looked at the auditorium doors. Could she actually walk through them and share a stage with Amber and Kyle after everything that had happened that day?

"Come on," said Megan, smiling hopefully. She pushed open the doors. "We'd better get in there now, or we'll *all* be in trouble."

Charlie sighed. She said nothing but took a deep breath and followed her friends.

The girls hurried up to the stage and took their places in the branches of Ian's freshly painted trees. They did look awesome — *better* than real somehow. Like dream trees, with wildly shaped leaves in colors nature had never thought of. And what was weird was that being in them made Charlie feel almost like she was in a different world, a world where maybe there were no embarrassing little sisters or mean eighth graders. They made her feel almost better. Now if she could just keep Alex from stepping on her hands . . .

Down below on the stage, Nicole looked up with a *Where were you?* expression, and Charlie replied with her own *I'll tell you later* face. In front of them both, Lenore was busy directing Amber and her ladies-in-waiting in their big — currently messy — dance routine.

"Ladies, *ladies!*" she said. "Remember, you are *noble*women. Please, no *hip* shaking! *Again.* From the top. And this time, let's add the *lyrics,* shall we?"

As they went through the moves again, Amber

opened her mouth and broke into song. It was all Charlie could do not to cover her ears.

"Cut! Cut! *Cut!*" Lenore bellowed. "Maid *Marian. Darling.* Your voice. Your *voice!* Be easy on your *instrument,* my dear. It's the *only* one you have. Strain it, and it may *very* well fail you."

Despite Lenore's warnings, and her fellow actors' winces, Amber continued to sing as loudly as she possibly could. For some reason, Amber was trying too hard — and it showed. She belted out her songs and paraded about the stage, casting frigid glares all the while into Charlie's tree.

Amber was *so* not herself, in fact, that she even forgot her lines. It was all Charlie could do not to whisper them to her. But no. She knew better! Charlie bit her lip and kept her squirrel face on as Amber muttered, "Line," again and again.

At last, and to everyone's relief, Lenore called an end to rehearsal early and gathered the cast around her for "a *most* exciting announcement!"

"I didn't want to *distract* anyone from *rehearsal,*" she said, rubbing her hands together, "but now I'd like to tell you all that your *costumes* are ready! Isn't it *wonderful?* I'd like to spend the *rest* of our rehearsal time trying them on. Do make yourselves *comfortable* in your characters' *clothes.* And we'll have a dress rehearsal *tomorrow!* Costumes, *please!*"

There were many happy murmurs as the eighth graders in charge of costumes walked out, arms piled high with their colorful creations. One girl, her arms full of veils and long dresses, headed toward Amber and her ladies-in-waiting. Two boys, carrying various shades of green and brown, walked over to Kyle and Nicole and the other Merry Men. Another eighth grade girl, bearing a stack of feathers and fur, made her way toward the woodland creatures. Charlie recognized her as one of Amber's friends, and she suddenly got a funny feeling in her stomach.

Looking rather bored, the girl handed out her lot, one by one, to all the animals.

"Skunk," she said, holding up a bushy black and white number.

"Oh! That's me!" said Claire. "This is going to be cute!"

"Raccoon," said the girl.

"Me!" said Megan.

Before long, just one costume was left. A thin, knowing smile inched its way across the eighth grade girl's face. "Squirrel," she said.

"Thanks," said Charlie. "That's me." She took the lump of brown fur.

"Don't mention it," the girl said, turning away with — could it be? — a giggle.

"Well, don't just *stand* there *looking* at your costumes!" declared Lenore. "*Go!* To the *restrooms*. Put them *on*! And be back in *exactly* ten minutes."

Exactly nine minutes later, Charlie stood in front of the bathroom mirror, wanting to cry — again!

"I look like a *rat*!" she wailed.

"No, you don't," said Nicole, sounding utterly *not* convincing.

"No," echoed Megan and Claire, sounding just as lame. "You don't look like a rat at all."

"Yes, I do!"

Everyone knew what squirrels looked like. They had big bushy tails. Charlie's was long and skinny. They had cute little ears. Hers were big and creepy. They had soft, fluffy fur. Hers was matted and greasy-looking. She didn't look anything like a squirrel. She looked like something people called exterminators for.

"Well, look at me," said Nicole. She pulled a floppy green hood over her head. "I look like a giant zucchini." She grinned and shrugged. "That's show business."

Charlie wanted to laugh, but she just couldn't.

Other people could, though.

"Ha, *ha*! How nice!" Amber strode up to Charlie's sink, dressed in a beautiful, long, blue and silver gown. "Big ears. Flat hair. Jane got your costume just right, didn't she? Now everyone in the audience will be able to recognize you right away!" She turned to the ladies-in-waiting, arranged like bridesmaids behind her, and paused to enjoy their supportive laughter. Then she looked over at Nicole and chuckled some more. "I just hope they don't think we're doing a Jolly Green Giant commercial!"

Charlie stood there, speechless. Nicole, however, had no trouble talking. She boldly stepped forward, her face level with Amber's tall, pointy, veiled headpiece. "Why do you have to be so mean?" she said. "We've never done anything to you."

"Whatever," said Amber, turning away and holding up her hand. "Come on, guys. Let's go."

And with a flip of her hair and a swish of her skirt, Amber whisked out the door, her attendants close behind.

"I hate her!" whispered Nicole.

"Me too," Megan and Claire agreed.

But Charlie said nothing. Instead, she tore off her ears and began peeling off her fur.

"What are you doing?" asked Claire. "Why are you taking your costume off?"

"Because," said Charlie, doing her best to keep it together. She wiped a paw across her eyes, smearing her hot, wet rat tears. "I'm done. No way am I going out there like this. And no way am I dealing with *her* anymore."

"But, Charlie!" said Nicole.

"We need you, remember?" said Megan.

"It's so obvious," said Claire, "that she's just jealous of you."

"Totally," said Nicole. "I mean, you sang way better than her yesterday. *And* Kyle's way more into . . ."

But Charlie stopped her by raising her paw. "Whatever," she said. She sincerely doubted that Amber was jealous — but even so, she didn't care. It just wasn't worth it.

"Where's my sister?" Charlie asked with a sniffle. "I've really got to go."

Scene 15

Hanging in There

Megan found Olivia helping Ian build the castle set, and delivered her to Charlie, who was waiting by the front door.

"We're going to tell Lenore you got sick and threw up," Nicole told her. "We're *not* going to tell her you're quitting."

"Fine," said Charlie, who didn't want to talk about it anymore. She tucked her furry ball of a costume under one arm, then grabbed Olivia by the hand and headed for home.

"Did you really throw up?" Olivia looked up at Charlie as she trotted along beside her. "Are you going to again?" she asked hopefully.

"Maybe," said Charlie, keeping her eyes focused on the sidewalk in front of her. There were still puddles left from the pouring rain the day before, and she trudged, on purpose, through as many as she could.

"Did you cry, too?" Olivia went on. "You look like you've been crying. Why were you crying? Did it hurt? Is that your costume? It looks cool! Can I try it on? You're not going to quit, are you? What was Nicole talking about, anyway? Do you know?"

"Look," groaned Charlie, who just wanted desperately to be home. "Can't you just be quiet? Can't you talk to Nelson or something, and leave me — and people like *Kyle* — alone?"

Olivia was quiet for a moment. She turned her head to the side, shook it a few times, and nodded. Then she peered back up at Charlie.

"Nelson says we're sorry about that," she said softly. "And he says you shouldn't quit. You don't even give him a headache anymore." She rolled her eyes. "But that Amber sure does!"

A few minutes later, Charlie was home. She'd been hoping to find the house empty, as it should be on a Tuesday afternoon. But no such luck. In fact, not only were Jen and Gwen home from cheerleading practice, but they'd invited all twenty members of their squad over, too. They seemed to be working on some kind of a bake sale project in the kitchen, and though the smell was appealing, the squeals and cheers were unbearable already.

Sean, meanwhile, had returned from his guitar lesson with two other students who were now trying to outdo each other with simultaneous solos.

"It's okay, Nelson," said Olivia as they walked in the door. "We'll play upstairs. Bye, Charlie."

As Olivia hurried off, Charlie dropped her backpack and pulled out her lump of a costume. It looked like roadkill in her hands. *I could throw up,* she thought as she tried to choke down the painful lump in her throat. Her lip curled in disgust. *There's just one place for this thing,* she told herself, heading back out the door.

Charlie walked through the garage to where they kept the garbage cans, and lifted the top of the big green one in the middle. She didn't even notice that her mom's car was in the garage until the car door opened.

"Hi, Charlie. What are you doing?"

"Mom!" said Charlie. You're home!"

Her mom laughed. "My class was cancelled," she explained. "There was some flooding, I guess, from the rain yesterday, and it messed up the wiring in the business science building. We might even have to cancel classes tomorrow." She smiled brightly.

"Too bad!" She closed the door of her car and locked it with a *bloop*. "So, what do you have there?"

Charlie looked at her bundle of mangy fur. "It's my costume," she muttered.

"What?" Her mom quickly walked over. "Why are you throwing away your costume?"

"Because I'm not going to be in the show."

"What do you mean? What happened?"

"Oh, Mom . . . I don't want to talk about it." Charlie sighed and her heart beat a little faster. There was more she wanted to say, but she bit her lip to stop. Why bother? "I don't see why you care so much, anyway," she blurted. "I mean, I know Jen and Gwen and Sean aren't interested. But if you're not going, what's the point?"

"What?" Her mom looked puzzled. "It's on Friday, isn't it? Of course I'm going."

Huh? Now Charlie was the puzzled one. "But it's not on your calendar."

"Which one?" her mother asked. "You mean the one in the kitchen?" She smiled and pulled a slim silver PA out of her bag. "That thing's just to keep track of who needs to be picked up and dropped off when," she said. "This is where I keep all of the *important* information."

Charlie's mouth fell open.

Her mom scrolled down to Friday and held the

screen up. "See? So tell me," she went on, "is that the *only* reason you didn't want to do the show? Or is there something else?"

Charlie sighed again. "There's this girl. She's in eighth grade. She made fun of me even *before* the show. But now . . . she's in the show, too. She has the best lines, and the greatest songs. But she makes me feel just awful, Mom. And she gets all the other eighth graders behind her and . . ."

A fresh wave of misery swept over her, and Charlie squeezed her tear-filled eyes tight. At last, she sniffed, held up the costume, and shook it out for her mom to see. "And then she had a friend of hers make *this* for me. Look at it! It's awful! And trust me, it's even worse on." She tossed the costume onto the car hood. "And that's why I'm not doing this stupid, *stupid* play."

Charlie's mom reached out and wrapped her arms around her. "Oh, sweetie, I'm so sorry." She hugged Charlie hard, then pulled back to look her in the eye. "What is it with bullies? Why do they have to ruin everything?" She shook her head. "I'll tell you one thing, though. If you let them win, they'll never stop. And if you drop out of the show because of this girl, I guarantee you she'll just keep on teasing you."

"That's kind of what Nicole says," said Charlie.

"Well, I want to tell you something else," said her mom, lifting her chin up gently. "You made a commitment to this show. And you wouldn't just be cheating me out of a Friday night out. You'd be letting the whole cast down."

Charlie rolled her eyes. "I'm just a squirrel."

Her mom lowered her head a fraction. "You took on this role and you need to see it through. And really, honey, deep down, don't you *want* to be in the show?"

"Well, yeah." Charlie nodded. "When Amber's not bothering me, it's fun." Then her eyes fell on the brown pile lying on the car. "But *not* in that!"

Her mom reached for the costume. "Hmm," she said. "You know, I never met a costume that couldn't be fixed." She held it up for closer inspection. "I bet with a little work, we could make you the cutest squirrel Sherwood Forest has ever seen. Come on. Let's go inside and see what we can do."

Suddenly, the front door swung open and Jen's perky head poked out.

"Charlie! There you are! Phone for you. It's Nicole. She said it was *urgent*. Oh, and, Mom! Don't worry about the smoke. We just burned some cookies — but it's all under control. I think Sean broke the lamp in the living room, though. Hurry up already, Charlie!"

Scene 16

Dress Rehearsal

By the time Charlie got off the phone with Nicole — after telling her not to worry, she was not going to quit the show — her mom had already started whipping her costume into shape.

"The broken lamp can wait until tomorrow," she said, clearly trying not to grit her teeth. "But no more guitars in the living room, Sean!"

Olivia donated some old stuffed animals Nelson had never liked anyway to the costume cause, and Charlie's mom produced a hideous fake fur bedspread she'd always *hoped* would come in handy. By bedtime, they had turned Charlie's pathetic costume into a healthy-looking, if not exactly adorable, squirrel.

"Thanks, Mom," Charlie said as she headed to

school the next morning. "You're the best." She gave her a big hug, and her mom squeezed her in return.

"Anytime," said her mom. She stood back and swept a stray piece of Charlie's hair behind her ear. "And *you're* the best for not quitting. It's hard, I know, but you won't be sorry." She kissed Charlie's nose. "Have a great day, okay?"

Charlie nodded. "Thanks. I'll try."

The school day passed slowly, until chorus, which seemed to fly by. Mr. Matthews had them sing a bunch of songs from the show, and Charlie realized how happy she was that she hadn't dropped out. She knew every song, even the ones she didn't have to sing. Now that her costume was decent, she was really looking forward to getting dressed up and — hopefully — having fun.

Not surprisingly, Amber quickly sought her out at dress rehearsal, her glare as nasty as ever. But what *was* surprising (and gratifying, too!) was the look on Amber's face after Charlie had changed into her costume. Charlie could tell right away that the improvements drove Amber absolutely crazy!

"You look *too* cute!" said Claire.

"Did your mom do all that?" asked Megan.

"Did you see Amber's face?" Claire went on. "Now, if we could just tweak *her* costume a little . . ."

Megan laughed.

"You know what, guys?" said Charlie, staunchly adjusting her ears. "Everything about this musical is awesome except Amber. So let's just let her do her thing and we'll do ours. Okay?"

Her friends nodded. "Okay."

"Plus," Charlie added, grinning, "it's not every day that we get to see Nicole and the other Merry Men in feathered hats and tights. We should enjoy it!" The girls all laughed.

"Places, everyone. *Places!*" Lenore suddenly called. She clapped her hands together briskly. "Woodland creatures, into your *trees*. I trust the *squirrel* is feeling better?" She peered over that day's mauve reading glasses at Charlie, who quickly nodded.

"Merry Men and peasants, into the *forest,*" she went on. "Noblemen *and* women, I need you in the wings. *Now,* people. *Now!* Robin Hood. Take your mark at center stage, if you *please*. We're going to take this from the *top* and go *all* the way through." She inhaled deeply and flung a long, lacy black sleeve toward Mr. Matthews. "William. Music, *please*. And . . . *begin!*"

"Brav-*o*! Brav-*o*!" Lenore ran onto the stage as soon as the last scene was over, clapping and crowing as if Oprah had just given her a car. "Well done! Well *done!*" She paused for a moment to refer to a little black notebook. "Just a few things: Little John! *Do* remember to stand *back* a little from Robin in the archery scene. You're going to get an arrow in the *face* if you're not careful. And Marian, *darling . . .*" She tucked the notebook under her arm and clasped her hands beseechingly before her. "Though I appreciate your *passion,* you're going to damage that *lovely* voice of yours if you aren't more *careful.* It should all come from the *diaphragm,* remember. The *diaphragm!*" She cleared her throat. "Like *this,* remember: mi, mi, mi, *miiiiii.*"

From her perch, Charlie looked down at Amber. She hadn't moved since the scene had ended, but her face had flushed several shades of red. She looked at Lenore and nodded, barely.

"Other than that —" Lenore opened her book again. "Prince *John*! Please remember to face the *audience* when you're plotting your dastardly deeds. I could *barely* hear you from my seat. Set dressers! Remind me to talk to you about *goblet* placement. And don't be *shy,* Friar Tuck! *Grab* that turkey leg when it's offered! Oh! Woodland *choir*! You sound absolutely *marvelous*! And aren't the sets just *gorgeous*?"

Lenore smiled and sighed like a proud, kind of scary stage mother. *She's right about the sets, though,* thought Charlie. *They do look amazing.*

"I think that just leaves us *one* more thing to go over before we finish." Lenore rubbed her hands together. "It's *my* personal favorite, and I'm sure it will soon be yours, too: *curtain* calls! Light crew, this is your time to *shine!*"

Lenore herded the whole cast to the front of the stage and arranged them in lines. As soon as she'd gotten the order *just* right (Robin Hood and Maid Marian in the middle, Prince John and the Sheriff of Nottingham beside them, then the nurse, Friar Tuck, Little John, and so on, until the line ended on one side with a white-tailed deer and on the other side with Charlie), Lenore had each pair of leads step up to take their bows.

Charlie stood and watched with a twinge of envy as the kids with speaking roles took their turns in the spotlight. *Next year,* she thought, *I'll be doing that, too.*

Then, at last, it was Amber and Kyle's turn. Clearly, any self-consciousness Amber might have felt before was now *long* forgotten. She took not one curtsy but three, practically poking poor Kyle's eye out with the tip of her pointy hat.

"Oops! Sorry!" Amber laughed. "You know," she said. "Maybe you should step back. . . ."

Kyle looked at her, clearly perplexed. "Huh?" He turned to Lenore.

"Er . . . yes . . . Amber, *darling,* what are you *saying*?"

"Oh, I'm just saying" — Amber shrugged *demurely,* as Lenore would say — "that after he walks me downstage, maybe he should just step back, you know, like, just a little, and let me take a curtsy on my own."

Kyle crossed his arms. "Hey! This is *Robin Hood.* And *I'm* Robin Hood."

"He does have a point, Marian, dear," Lenore added.

"Oh, fine." Amber tossed back her veil.

"Very good then. Cast!" Lenore made her own bow before them. "You are a *credit* to the *theater*! Go! *Change* out of your costumes. Be sure to go over your lines and songs again this evening. And I shall see you *tomorrow*! Remember! Be here one hour before showtime. You are responsible for your own warm-ups! And *don't* forget your *makeup!*"

Friday afternoon came like a lightning bolt — fast and full of energy, and just a little scary. Charlie might as well have sent a dummy to her classes for all she heard or said. Her mind was centuries away in Sherwood Forest, replaying every line and song in the entire school play.

The only things she did notice were the signs throughout the halls demanding that everyone come to the show that night. ROBIN HOOD WANTS YOU! one poster read. It showed a remarkable likeness of Kyle in his feathered green cap and caused more than a few girls to be late to class. It was one of several posters that Ian had been working on the week before, and Charlie was awfully impressed . . . and proud to say she knew the artist!

"I wonder," mused Nicole as they slowly walked by the poster on the way to math, "what'll happen to that poster after Saturday's performance. It sure would look good in my room. . . ."

Nicole had brought her costume in that morning so that she could go home with Charlie after school. She was still super-nervous about knowing all her lines and fully intended to run through them with Charlie *all* afternoon.

"You're so lucky to be in the chorus." Nicole sighed. "I mean, I don't even have *that* big a role, and it's so much pressure! Hey! I know! Trade with me! I mean, you know my part perfectly. I kind of know your songs. We'll switch, and once the curtain goes up, there's no way Lenore could stop us!"

Charlie laughed. "Uh, sorry!" she said. "You can't get out of this one so easily. Besides — like you could fit into my costume. You're way too tall." She laughed again. "And really, who would believe me as Little John?"

No, in fact, as much as Charlie had wanted a big, juicy role, and as much as she had envied Nicole and even Amber, she was surprisingly content to know she'd be in the background of the show. Her mom was coming, her name would be in the program (though probably as "Charlotte"), and she got to sing *and* go to the cast party afterward. The whole thing was fine — just *fine* with her.

Scene 17

Opening Night

When they got back to Charlie's house, the girls had a good half hour of practice time before Olivia got home.

"Well, that's it," said Charlie when she heard the door open. "We'll never get any peace now."

But to her amazement, Olivia left them alone. She did pop into their room once to ask if they wanted any water.

"Remember! Lenore says keep highlighted," she said.

"It's 'hydrated,'" said Charlie. "And no — uh, thanks — we're fine."

"Okay, then," said Olivia. "I'll be downstairs. You guys just stay up here and call me if you need anything. I'll come get you when it's time to go!"

"What about Nelson?" asked Charlie, surprised not to hear Olivia mention him at all.

"Hmm?" said Olivia, considering the question. "Don't know." She shrugged. "But don't worry. I'm sure he wouldn't miss your show!"

If that weren't odd enough, Jen and Gwen arrived home later without so much as a "rah-rah" or a "sis-boom-bah."

"Maybe they're sick?" Charlie said as she listened to the eerie silence. "Either that, or I'm losing my hearing."

Nicole shrugged. "Lucky us, I say. C'mon. Let's do that part from Scene Two. And want to see if Olivia can bring us up something to eat?"

At last, it was quarter to six — time to go. Charlie and Nicole gathered up their costumes and all the makeup they could find and, with Olivia, headed back to school.

They left Charlie's mom and older sisters eating dinner in the kitchen.

"Bye, hon. Bye, Nicole," called her mom. "Stay out of everyone's way, now, Olivia. See you all soon!"

"Break a leg!" Jen and Gwen yelled.

When they got to school, Olivia hurried off to find Lenore. The drama teacher had come to think of Olivia as her personal assistant and had promised to save lots of backstage work for her to do. Charlie and Nicole, meanwhile, headed to the girls' room to change into their costumes.

They could hear the excited squeals inside before they even got to the door. Just as Charlie reached for the thick, silver handle, the door swung open and Amber whisked out.

The scowl on her perfectly made-up face was intense and grew more so the minute she saw Charlie.

Charlie jumped back — literally — in anticipation of whatever nasty comment was sure to come. But none did.

Amber's mouth opened slightly but then clamped quickly shut. With a swoosh of her long lamé skirt, she marched away.

Charlie looked at Nicole, and they both shrugged.

Amber Wiley's strange preshow behavior, however, was soon forgotten as the girls walked through the door.

"What do you think?" asked Megan, turning from a mirror. "Too much black around my eyes? It's awful, isn't it? *Argh!* Do I have time to wash it off *again*?"

"Would you tell her to relax?" said Claire. "You

look great, Megan. We've got plenty of time, any-way. Hey! My *ears*! Where'd they go?"

Charlie quickly slipped into her own costume — brown tights and furry jumper, fluffyish tail and headband ears — then got to work on her face. She'd practiced the night before using the thick theatrical makeup to transform her own face into that of a squirrel. She thought it had turned out pretty well, all in all. The key, really, was the white around the mouth, and the shape of the nose. The hard part was not ending up looking like a dog.

Charlie gave her nose one more dab, then used her mom's eyeliner to draw in some whiskers. When she felt adequately squirrel-like, she turned to help Nicole with her beard.

"Come on! We'd better hurry!" shouted Claire.

"Does this look right?" Nicole asked, modeling her mascaraed chin. "Or does it look like I've got some weird tattoo on my face?"

"It's fine," said Megan. "Let's go!"

Leaving her street clothes and makeup where they were, Charlie slipped on her furry gloves and followed her friends out of the girls' room, through the backstage door, and into the wings, where the cast had already begun to gather. Half of them were doing various voice and body warm-ups. The other half were shooting fake arrows, stealing hats, and laughing like hyenas at the sight of boys in makeup. The only one not doing anything, it seemed, was Amber. She wasn't even flirting with Kyle, who was looking particularly dashing — even with blush and eye shadow.

"Just look at her," Nicole said, nodding bitterly in Amber's direction. "She thinks she's so much better than everybody else. I hope she falls on her face."

"Well, I don't," said Claire. "It would ruin the show. It'll be bad enough if she sounds like she has for these past few rehearsals."

Charlie had to agree. No matter how she felt about Amber, they'd all worked too hard on the show to see it be anything but perfect. That night they were a team, even Amber.

"Hey! Have you guys looked out there?" asked Alex, running back from the edge of the curtain. "It's packed!"

"Really?" Nicole asked. She looked at Charlie and made a face.

Bring it on! thought Charlie. She sang a bit of the woodland creatures' opening song, inspired by the orchestra, which was busily tuning up.

Just then, Olivia ran up bearing one very long, very red rose.

"For you!" she said, offering it up to Charlie.

"For me?" Charlie instantly felt every eye backstage upon her.

"Well, take it!" said Nicole.

"Read the note!" said Claire.

Sure enough, there was a card attached to the stem. Charlie opened the tiny envelope and slipped it out.

Nicole was already leaning over her shoulder to generously read the note for her.

To the cutest squirrel in Sherwood.
Break a leg tonight!
A Fan

"Oh, my gosh!" said Nicole, reading the note over her shoulder. "He really *does* like you!"

"Who?" asked Charlie, still staring at the card.

"Kyle, of course!" Nicole squealed.

"Do you *really* think so?" Charlie tried to look casual—as casual as a giant squirrel could—as she peered in Kyle's direction. He was staring curiously at the scene the girls had caused, and his smile widened a bit as his eyes met Charlie's.

Charlie caught her breath and read the note again.

"I mean, come on," said Nicole. "Who else could it be?"

"Well," Megan began. "You never know . . ."

"No, I know," said Nicole. "And I'll bet my hood he asks her to dance at the cast party tonight."

Charlie just smiled . . . and smiled and smiled and smiled. It was strange, though. It was like a dream come true, and yet the note didn't seem like something Kyle would do . . . at all.

"Look at Amber!" Nicole went on. "You *know* she's wondering where *her* rose is!"

Charlie looked over, but it was too late. Amber had already turned away.

"Fifteen minutes!" a voice called suddenly. "Fifteen minutes to curtain!"

Lenore Von Gugenberg entered the wings, wearing a long black dress and beaded black earrings that dangled below her shoulders. A black shawl with long, shiny fringe was draped over her arms, and a black silk scarf was tied like a turban around her head.

"Gather round, *cast,*" she called, the fringe on her shawl rippling wildly. "It's nearly showtime! Is everyone *hydrated?*"

"Yes!"

"*Wonderful!* Has everyone used the restroom?"

"Yes!"

"*Wonderful!* Let's hear a few la-ahhhhs and

la-ohhhhhs . . . from the diaphragm, now. From the *diaphragm,* remember!"

"Laaaaa-ahhhhhhhhhhhh."

"Laaaaa-ohhhhhhhhhhhh."

"*Wonderful!* I believe we are *ready!*"

She opened her eyes and looked at them warmly.

And then, suddenly, Amber was stepping forward, her hand raised and her head way, way down.

"Yes? Maid Marian? Would you like to *say* something? How *marvelous!* We're listening!"

Amber took a deep breath and slowly tilted her head up from the floor. Then she opened her mouth. A voice croaked out as if from an ancient, thirsty toad.

"I . . . I don't think I can sing."

Scene 18

In the Spotlight

The silence backstage was deafening.

Charlie didn't know which was worse: watching Lenore's face fall or watching it fire back up, like some wild, false-eyelashed maelstrom.

"*Excuse* me?" the drama teacher finally managed.

Amber opened her mouth again, but this time all that came out were a few creaky syllables and a raspy squawk or two.

Lenore's hand flew to her own mouth, where her teeth chomped down on the first knuckle they could find.

"This is . . . this is . . . *unprecedented*! This is . . . *horrifying*! This is . . . not *happening*! Olivia! Olivia! A *chair*!"

Olivia slid a chair in behind Lenore just in time

to catch her. Her arms fell down and her head fell back and she sat there, not moving, for what seemed like a very long time.

And then, as if someone suddenly flipped a switch inside her, Lenore sat up, her eyebrows high, and hungrily looked around. At last, her eyes fell like a net upon Charlie.

"You! *Charlotte!* What are you *waiting* for? Get out of that rat suit right *now* and into Amber's costume. Tonight, you are *Maid Marian*! Amber, you'll wear Charlotte's costume and at least fill in the background. Now, people! *Now!*" She rose from her chair and threw her shawl over her shoulder. "The *show* must go *on!*"

Charlie, meanwhile, stood frozen in place. *What?* she thought. Did Lenore just say *she* would be Maid Marian? (And did her costume *still* really look like a rat?)

"C'mon, Charlie! Hurry!" Nicole had grabbed her arm and was pulling her toward the door. "You heard her. You've got to change!"

With an expression truly tragic, Amber followed along behind them, back into the bathroom. Within minutes, Amber and Charlie stood staring at each other in each other's costumes. It was almost, Charlie thought, like their heads had been switched. It could not have been any weirder.

She was about to say something to Amber, some-thing about being so sorry she lost her voice; about how she shouldn't worry, it was sure to be back the next day; about how her squirrel ears were just a little crooked, and could she *please* tell Charlie if there was still squirrel makeup on her face? But she never got the chance. Amber had turned and was out the door before Charlie could say a word.

Charlie winced as the door slammed shut on Amber's tail and she roughly yanked it free.

"Well?" said Nicole, poking her hooded head through the door. "What are you waiting for?"

"I don't think I can do this!" Charlie choked.

"Of course you can!" Nicole stepped into the girls' room. "You know every line and every song in the whole play."

"But what if I forget in front of all those people?" Charlie could just see that horrible, terrible, miser-able audition thing happening again. It had been bad enough in front of other kids who were trying out. She could only imagine how mortifying it would be in front of most of the school *and* a whole bunch of strangers!

Nicole swung her bow behind her back and grabbed Charlie by the shoulders. "You can do it," she said. "And you will. Remember how great you were playing Maid Marian in rehearsal?"

Charlie nodded.

"And remember what you told me? How everything around you melted away?"

Charlie nodded again.

"So, let that happen again tonight. I mean, just forget about everything else. And if you can't, imagine the audience in their underwear or something."

Charlie laughed — a little.

"Oh, my gosh! And then there's *this*." Nicole reached for the rose Charlie had set down on the sink.

Charlie looked at her, puzzled.

"Kyle!" said Nicole. "It's like a sign — you know, that you were meant to be together!"

Was it really? Charlie felt numb. She just didn't know. . . .

"Just repeat after me." Nicole looked her square in the eye. "I, Charlie Moore."

"I, Charlie Moore."

"By the powers vested in me."

"By the powers vested in me."

"Do solemnly swear."

"Do solemnly swear."

"To sing like a superstar."

"To sing like a superstar."

"And show Amber."

"And show Amber."

"That sixth graders rule."

"That sixth graders rule."

Just then, Olivia's head poked through the door. "Five minutes," she said. "Lenore's looking for you. Wow, Charlie! You look pretty!"

Charlie looked at her sister and smiled. "Okay. Let's go."

She could already hear Lenore onstage, announcing, "This *evening,* the role of Maid *Marian* will be *played* by Charlotte Moore. . . ."

The curtain rose, but Charlie wasn't behind it; she wouldn't come on until halfway through the first scene. She stood in the wings, among her eighth grade ladies-in-waiting — terrified to look at them! — and concentrated hard on the action onstage instead.

Kyle was walking across the stage, pretending to shoot arrows with Will Scarlett, while in the background the woodland creatures sang their opening song. Charlie could see Amber perched in a tree, mouthing the words and looking completely miserable.

Nicole hadn't gone on yet, either, but her entrance would come from the other side of the stage. She stood there now, waving and sending all kinds of soundless words of encouragement Charlie's way.

Charlie nodded back, then closed her eyes and tried to remember how it was, exactly, that one breathed.

What if she forgot her lines? She knew them. She really did. But she'd never actually said them all together, all the way through.

Or what if she missed her marks — she'd certainly never walked through the whole play! — and messed up everyone else's lines and marks, too?

What if she spent the rest of junior high school known as the biggest fool in school?

Charlie jumped as she felt a hand on her sleeve.

"M'lady?" It was Prince John.

She took his arm and braced herself for her clearly unavoidable entrance.

"I can do this," she said quickly, intending it only for herself. But it came out much more loudly than she had planned.

Bellamy, the lady-in-waiting standing directly behind her, leaned over and expertly fluffed Charlie's silvery veil. "We know you can," she said.

Charlie didn't even have time to be surprised by Bellamy's kind words. It was showtime!

On Prince John's arm, Charlie stepped out into the spotlight.

Remarkably, from her very first line, the words and songs flowed out just as they were supposed to. (The hardest part was not singing her squirrel songs, too!) After her first scene, Charlie saw Olivia give her a thumbs-up from the wings, and it was smooth sailing from there. Even Kyle's dreamy smiles didn't make her nervous. If anything, they made her feel more like Maid Marian than ever!

For an hour and a half, Charlie *was* a noble maiden in medieval England, in love with an outlaw and willing to risk her life to save him. The blue and silver dress and pointy hat she wore were *hers*. The songs she sang were *hers*. Even the dances she'd always thought were a little goofy were *hers*.

And then, just as suddenly as it had all begun, the curtain was coming down, and a thunder of applause was sounding from the other side. Quickly, Charlie ran toward the wings to take her place at the end of the curtain call line, just like in rehearsal. Only after Kyle had chased her down did she remember that, for that night, she'd take her bow in a different place — center stage.

Kyle took one hand, and Prince John the other, and they waited, grinning, as the curtain was raised.

Charlie looked out at the crowd and her mouth fell open. Had all those people been watching her? *Really?* There were a ton of them! And they were all standing up. Each and every one. *And* clapping *and* whistling *and* yelling out her name!

"Charlie! Yeah, Charlie!" Plus some *"Yeah, Charlotte!s,"* too.

More than a bit dazed, Charlie let her hands be raised, then brought down in a deep bow, and raised again above her head.

Suddenly, a familiar whistle cut through her haze. *Mom?* Charlie searched to find her and finally did — there, in her favorite white sweater, a few rows back from the stage. Right next to her — you couldn't miss them! — were a pair of giant Day-Glo signs.

GO!

CHARLIE!

The signs dropped down a little, revealing Jen's and Gwen's beaming twin faces.

"CHAR-*LIE*!" they yelled.

Charlie couldn't believe that they were there! And wait! Was that *Sean* standing beside them? Hadn't *he* said he'd rather be dead than come to some dumb school show? And was he really clapping?

The cast took one more bow as a group before they broke into pairs, as Lenore had shown them. Charlie clapped for her friends as she waited breathlessly for her turn.

At last, Kyle took her hand and led her out to center stage, and the applause hit a new high.

Charlie almost fell back, especially when Kyle stepped back to clap for her, too.

Overwhelmed by the ovation, Charlie turned to her fellow cast members, hoping they could take some of the attention away. But when she turned around, they were all applauding! Nicole, still in character, was whistling through her teeth, but everyone else down the line was smiling and clapping — even, to Charlie's amazement, the brown-furred squirrel at the end.

And then, the next thing Charlie knew, Olivia was walking out from the wings, this time with a bouquet of flowers almost as big as she was. As she took the flowers from her sister, Charlie didn't know if she wanted to curtain to come down and save her, or if she wanted the applause to go on and on and on. All she knew was that life could not possibly get any better!

Scene 19

The Grand Finale

"Ladies and *Gentlemen,* I'd like to propose a toast!"

Charlie looked up from the couch she was sharing with Megan and Nicole to see Lenore Von Gugenberg raising a plastic cup of red punch. She had hit her mark, halfway up her own staircase, and was gazing out proudly over her houseful of kids. Everyone was there for the after-show cast party: actors, musicians, stage crew. Everyone, that is, but Amber.

"I *said,* I'd like to propose a *toast!*"

Slowly, the bubbly crowd's attention turned to Lenore.

She nodded. "To *Charlotte!*" She raised her empty hand and let it glide toward Charlie. "Without whom this *show* would not have been *possible* tonight."

The room filled with cheers, and Charlie could feel her cheeks turn the same color as Lenore's punch.

"I *do* trust," Lenore went on, "that with a good night's rest, our *darling* Amber will be able to *resume* her role tomorrow. *But,* Charlotte, I *must* tell you, there may *never* be, in the *history* of the *theater,* a performance as *bold* and *heroic* as yours. *Truly!* I can say with *utmost* authority, a *star* has been *born!*"

With that, Lenore tossed back her head and drank her punch in one long gulp. *"Enjoy!"* she said, blotting her chin with the end of her shawl.

The crowd clapped some more, and Nicole gave Charlie a hug.

"Did you hear that? A *star!*"

Charlie blushed some more and shook her head. "Enough already!" she said. But inside she was thinking, *I could get used to all this!*

"I still can't believe you knew that whole part!" said Megan. "But I do hope you're back in the chorus tomorrow." She pouted. "We need you!"

Just then, Claire came running over. "Guys! You've got to see this! I think there are real *awards* in Lenore's dining room. What's a Tony? Do you know?"

"Are you serious?" Megan jumped up. "Show me!"

Once they'd gone, Nicole turned back to Charlie. "I've got to know," she said in a breathless whisper, leaning closer. "What was it like?"

"What?"

"To be that close to Kyle." Nicole bit her lip and sighed. "I mean, you were probably breathing his *air*! What was it like? What was it like to hold his hand?"

"Oh." Charlie giggled. *That.* She'd been thinking about that, a little. But, to her surprise, not in the way she'd expected. She'd been thinking, actually, about how *little* she thought about it.

"I don't know." Charlie shrugged. "Honestly, I have to tell you, his hands were kind of . . . sweaty. I mean, I know he was probably nervous . . ." Though he really hadn't seemed nervous at all. "But . . . it was kind of . . . not that exciting."

Nicole frowned. "Are you kidding?"

Charlie shook her head and watched as Nicole examined her own palms.

"You know, my hands are pretty sweaty. . . . ," said Nicole.

Charlie rolled her eyes. "It was just an observation. I guess what I'm saying is that Kyle is really nice, and, of course, super-cute, but he wasn't actually the best part of the show for me."

She could tell it wasn't easy for Nicole to process this information, and to Nicole's credit, the facts didn't seem to add up. Fact: Kyle could not have been nicer to her. Fact: Kyle was gorgeous. Fact: Charlie didn't really want to hold his hand. But facts were facts. What could she do?

"So, what did you do with the rose?" asked Nicole, still recovering from mild shock. "And what are you going to do if he asks you to go out with him?"

"Well, first of all," said Charlie, "my mom won't let me 'go out' yet. But . . ." She'd been thinking about this a little, too. What if that rose *was* from Kyle? She'd thought it had to be from her mom at first. Why would *Kyle* give her a flower? But then Olivia had delivered that huge bouquet from her family at the end of the show. So the rose wasn't from her mom. Who else could it have been from?

What if Kyle really did like her?

"Hey."

Charlie and Nicole both looked up, open-mouthed, to see Kyle grinning before them. Though he was back in regular clothes, he was still wearing his Robin Hood cap. He took it off and bowed just like he had done in the show.

The girls turned to each other, then back to Kyle again. With an eyebrow raise to Charlie, Nicole slid off the couch and onto her feet.

No! thought Charlie. *Don't leave me here alone!*

"I was just going to get some punch," Nicole said. She took a step back and smiled shyly.

"Oh, okay." Kyle looked at his hat, and Charlie quickly noticed that his perfect dimples seemed to fade. "I was just going to ask you if you wanted to dance."

"Huh?" Nicole froze, and Charlie did, too. "Who? *Me?*"

Kyle shrugged and the dimple on his right side reappeared. "Yeah, *you*." He smiled at Nicole, then glanced at Charlie as if to ask, *Is your friend okay?*

Charlie smiled and shrugged right back.

"Go ahead," Charlie told her, doing her own eyebrow raise. "I'll bring you some punch later."

Nicole's eyes widened.

"You heard her." Kyle reached for Nicole's hand, and Charlie could almost see her best friend's heart leap in her chest. "Besides, you're one of my Merry Men. You have to do what I say. Oh!" He flashed one of his best and brightest dimpled smiles once more at Charlie. "Awesome job, again!" he said.

Then Nicole waved (and wiped her sweaty hand

quickly on her jeans) and Charlie watched Kyle lead her off to the back porch, where music was playing and lots of kids were dancing.

So, she thought, sitting back to take in her surroundings, *this is where Lenore lives.* It was certainly . . . dramatic. Big colorful paintings filled the walls. And there were flowers — gobs of them — everywhere she looked. There were silk ones, dried ones, china ones, you name it. And, of course, lots of fresh ones. Roses seemed to be Lenore's favorite.

Charlie's mind returned to the rose from her mystery fan. It was clear now that it couldn't have come from Kyle. He was Nicole's fan, not hers! But if not Kyle, then . . . who?

"Hi, Charlie."

"Hm?" Charlie looked up. "Oh, hi!" It was Ian. "Looking for Megan? She was in the dining room, I think."

He shook his head. "No."

"Oh?"

"Mind if I sit down?"

"Uh . . . sure."

Charlie scooted over happily to make more room. Ian was *always* nice to talk to — and yet, Charlie suddenly realized, she wasn't sure where to begin.

"So I —"

"I just —"

They both laughed apologetically.

"You first," said Charlie.

"No, no, you."

"Well," Charlie began. "I just wanted to tell you your sets looked really awesome. Amazing, really. I meant to tell you before, but things have been so crazy."

"Thanks," he said. He looked honestly flattered. Then he leaned in and whispered, "But you know, it was all Nelson."

Charlie laughed, enjoying the joke.

Ian glanced down at his lap, then lifted his eyes a little shyly. "I wanted to tell *you* that you were great." He grinned. "I mean, I guess you know that. No one else could have filled in for Amber like you did. Of course, if you ask me, you should have been Maid Marian from the beginning."

Wow, thought Charlie. Of all the nice things people had said to her that night, none had made her feel so . . . well, so good. She looked into Ian's smiling gray eyes and felt a sudden tingle roll through her. Then she took a *very* self-conscious breath and tried to blink.

"I'm glad you weren't, though," he went on. "I got to talk to you a lot more. What can I say?" He shrugged. "I'm a fan."

Charlie's jaw dropped open. Then she turned and peered at him out of the corner of her eye.

"You?" she said, maybe a little too loudly. Giggling, she dropped her head, sure that everyone else in the room could see her blushing. "Really?" she whispered. "*You* sent me the rose?"

"Yeah," Ian whispered back. "Cheesy, right? I just thought you deserved it."

Charlie looked at him, wishing that she could do something other than smile.

"So," said Ian, with a nod toward Lenore's porch. "I see your friend Nicole's out there dancing with Kyle."

"Uh-huh." Charlie swallowed.

"Do you want to, maybe, dance, too? Or . . ." He made a kind of cute, kind of silly face. ". . . do you want to sit here and analyze Lenore's artwork?"

Charlie sighed and grinned, as happy and as comfortable as she had been that night onstage. "Both," she said. "Why don't we start by you telling me what you think of that painting over there, the one with the red and purple . . . blobs."

Ian laughed and reached for her hand. "That one happens to be my favorite. . . ."

About the Author

Lara Bergen made her own junior high school musical debut as a Flying Monkey in Robert Frost Middle School's production of *The Wizard of Oz* (in which she was politely asked to mouth her lyrics instead of sing them). This was, undoubtedly, influential in her decision to move to New York City to pursue writing . . . and avoid karaoke whenever possible.

check out

The Babysitting Wars

by MiMi MCCoy
Another
candy apple book . . .
just for you.

Kaitlyn started off down the corridor, cradling her stack of books in her arms. Fortunately, the hall wasn't too crowded. She would be able to see Topher's locker from a distance, so she could time their "chance" meeting.

There he was, alone at his locker, just like she'd hoped he would be.

Ooh! He was so cute! She quickened her pace.

Soon Kaitlyn was only a few feet away. She was about to begin her leisurely stroll through Topher's line of vision when suddenly, from out of nowhere, a girl swooped in right under her nose.

It was Nola.

As Kaitlyn watched, Nola began to talk to Topher. From the way Nola was standing, leaning in close to him, Kaitlyn could tell she didn't want anyone else to hear what they were saying. Kaitlyn couldn't guess what they were talking about, but it was pretty obvious that they had more than a three-word relationship.

Topher handed Nola a folded-up sheet of paper. Nola gave a little nod, like she was agreeing to something. Then she turned and walked away.

Kaitlyn stared after her, confused. What had just happened? How did Nola know Topher? And what was on that folded-up piece of paper?

Suddenly Kaitlyn realized that she was still standing in the middle of the hallway. Kids were passing on her left and right. She shook herself and continued on to class.

In Spanish class, Kaitlyn waited for Topher to turn around, but he never did. For the rest of the day, Kaitlyn's thoughts swirled around Topher and Nola. They had acted so secretive. But Nola had been at school for less than a week. What kind of secret could she possibly have with Topher? Unless . . .

Could Nola *like* Topher?

Worse thought: Could Topher like *Nola*?

By the time Kaitlyn got home from school that day, she felt exhausted from thinking about it.

Kaitlyn's mother was sitting at the kitchen table, talking on the phone. Mrs. Sweeney was head of the

Parent-Teacher Association at Lily's school, and she spent a lot of time talking to other parents. She called it "networking." Kaitlyn called it "gossiping."

Kaitlyn took a carton of milk out of the fridge, poured herself a glass, and got a stack of sandwich cookies from a jar on the counter. She carried her snack over to the table.

Mrs. Sweeney finished her conversation and hung up. "Hi, sweetie," she said to Kaitlyn. "How was school?"

"Fine," Kaitlyn replied automatically.

"Are you babysitting tonight, honey? I was just talking to the Nichols down the street. They need a sitter, if you're free."

"I *wish* I were free," Kaitlyn groaned. "But I already said I'd sit for the Monster."

Her mother's forehead wrinkled. "Who?"

Oops. Kaitlyn had never told her mother her nickname for Mrs. Arnold's kid. "Troy Arnold," she said quickly.

"Oh?" Mrs. Sweeney looked surprised. "I thought you said you'd never sit for them again."

Kaitlyn rolled her eyes. "Momentary lapse of reason."

"Well, in that case, the Nichols want to know if you've heard of another sitter — someone named Nola?"

Kaitlyn choked on her cookie. She grabbed her glass of milk and took a huge gulp.

"They say they've been hearing great things about her," Mrs. Sweeney went on, apparently not noticing that her daughter had almost inhaled an entire Oreo. "She has all these wonderful ways of entertaining kids. . . . Are you all right, honey?"

"Just went down the wrong pipe," Kaitlyn said hoarsely. She wiped her watering eyes with the back of her hand.

"Don't eat so fast," her mother advised. "So, do you know this girl, Nola?"

"There's a new girl at school named Nola," Kaitlyn said cautiously. "I don't really know her, though. Um, what did the Nichols say about her?"

"Well, apparently she's done some sitting for the Browns and the Parkers and the Davises, and everyone was very happy with her."

The Browns and the Parkers and the Davises? Those were *her* customers!

Kaitlyn stood up from the table.

"What's wrong?" her mother asked.

"I have to go make some calls," Kaitlyn said, already halfway out the door.

Something weird is going on, she thought as she stormed up the stairs to her bedroom. *And I'm going to get to the bottom of it.*